"I'm about to remedy my bride's neglect."

He fastened strong fingers around Zoe's fragile wrist and drew her to her feet. Her elusive, utterly tantalizing perfume made his head spin. The warmth of her sensuous body as she fluidly closed the space between them sent a shaft of driving need through his nervous system, the force of it rocking him back on his heels.

This was about sex. He knew it and she knew it.

It was there in the hazy glow of her golden eyes, the rapid pulse beat at the base of her long creamy throat, the wild rose color that stole across her cheeks, the erect nipples angled against his chest just below his thundering heart. It was there in the quiver of heated flesh beneath slinky silk as he scooped her into his arms, and, tossing the words over his shoulder as he walked through the doorway, he said, "I know you'll excuse us. My wife and I have some serious remedying to do."

Diana Hamilton

A SPANISH MARRIAGE

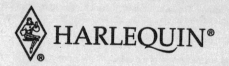

HARLEQUIN®

TORONTO • NEW YORK • LONDON
AMSTERDAM • PARIS • SYDNEY • HAMBURG
STOCKHOLM • ATHENS • TOKYO • MILAN • MADRID
PRAGUE • WARSAW • BUDAPEST • AUCKLAND

ISBN 0-373-12399-X

A SPANISH MARRIAGE

First North American Publication 2004.

Copyright © 2004 by Diana Hamilton.

PROLOGUE

'MUST you leave us tomorrow, Javier? We don't see nearly enough of you. Your father and I go to the coast in one week, as you know. Spend it here with us? Just one more week of your time; it's not too much to ask?'

'Sorry, Mama.' Genuine regret darkened Javier Masters' smoke-grey eyes as he accepted his mother's huff of exasperation. In her mid-fifties Isabella Maria was still the dark-haired, proud-eyed Spanish beauty his English father had fallen fathoms-deep in love with thirty years ago when he had been in his mid-forties and, so he often said, had resigned himself to never finding a woman he could contemplate spending the rest of his life with.

Isabella Maria drew herself stiffly upright in her brocaded chair. 'Hah! So much for your always saying how much you love being here!'

A log fell in the huge stone hearth, sending sparks flying. Javier unfolded his long legs, left the squashy confines of the sofa and went to tend the fire, a necessary indulgence now that the cold winds from the snow-capped peaks of the Sierra Nevada heralded the approach of winter. His father's, 'Don't nag the boy, Izzy,' brought a wry smile to his flattened mouth as he accepted the truth of what his mother had said.

He'd loved this place as soon as he'd set his fascinated eyes on it as a seven-year-old when his parents had bought it as a holiday home. A former Moorish caravanserai, it lay in the heart of the tiny Andalucian town behind a stout studded door, the building arcaded around a flagged courtyard, which in summer was filled with the heady scents of roses, myrtle and lilies.

Since his father's retirement and health problems his parents had transferred the family home, Wakeham Lodge in Gloucestershire, to him and spent the summers here but left for their home on the coast when winter pressed down from the mountains, remaining there until after the Easter celebrations.

'There's nothing I'd like better than to stay on,' he admitted as he straightened and took a straddle-legged position in front of the hearth, his wide shoulders lifting in a resigned shrug beneath the fine black cashmere that moulded his impressive torso. 'But I have a problem.'

'The business?' Lionel Masters put in sharply. He had retired three years ago, handing over the reins to his only son, but he still took a keen interest in the construction business he and his one-time partner Martin Rothwell had founded and brought to impressive success, now a world beater in Javier's more than capable hands.

'Nothing like that,' he quickly put his father's mind at rest, adding drily, 'Business problems I can handle. But this one goes by the name of Zoe Rothwell.'

Two simultaneous expressive 'Aah!'s were followed by a silence so intense Javier could hear his heart beating. Heavily.

He glanced at the slim gold-banded watch he wore on his flat wrist. In roughly fifteen minutes Solita, the resident housekeeper, would announce that dinner was served. Best spell it out, get it over with.

'Yesterday, as I was leaving a meeting in Madrid I received a call from Alice Rothwell on my mobile. She sounded at the end of her tether and—to leave out the histrionics—it boils down to a blunt demand that I take over Zoe's guardianship because Alice can't and won't cope any longer.'

'And?' Isabella Maria arched fine black brows and laid a dramatic hand on her silk-clad breast. 'How could Alice think this is possible? I always thought she was a strange old woman—so cold and prim and proper—and now we add madness to the catalogue! Why should she think you can care for her little granddaughter? It would be different if you had a wife. But you do not.'

Registering the latent disapproval in that last statement, Javier caught his father's grin and gave back a wry shrug. As an only child his confirmed bachelorhood had been Isabella Maria's greatest anxiety since he had reached the age of twenty-five three years ago. His mother wanted grandchildren; there was the future generation to think of—well, wasn't there?

But Javier was nowhere near ready to tie himself down; he enjoyed his male freedom far too much. He worked damned hard so he was entitled to play hard. He enjoyed women, lovely, sophisticated creatures who shared his view that only an immature fool could mistake old-fashioned lust for love.

'Zoe can no longer be classed as a child,' Javier

pointed out at last, ignoring the barb about his wife-less state. 'She's sixteen. The worst kind of bolshie teenager, according to her grandmother. Apparently, she is now flatly refusing to return to boarding-school, skulking around the house, playing loud music at all hours of the day and night, giving Alice a load of grief. Which she wants to hand over to me,' he ended drily.

'Why you?' Lionel Masters regarded his son over steepled fingers. 'You're already a corporate legend,' he commented proudly. 'A tough operator but fair, the original iron fist in a velvet glove. The responsibility of a tricky teenage girl wouldn't cause you to lose a second's worth of sleep, so I can see the way Alice's mind would be working. But there is no blood relationship, no family duty Alice Rothwell has a right to call on.'

Javier's handsome mouth tightened. 'There's a moral duty. Dating from when Zoe's father sold his share in the business to you and then died with her mother, Grace, in that house fire six weeks later,' he reminded coolly. 'Thankfully, Zoe was staying with a school friend and was spared, but that night she lost both her parents, her home, all the security an eight-year-old girl had ever known. I felt deeply sorry for both Alice and Zoe and I thought someone from our family should take an interest,' he emphasised bluntly.

'Alice Rothwell's not the easiest woman to like.' He spread his hands dismissively. 'That aside, her husband had died the year before, she'd lost her son and was landed with a granddaughter she found impossible to handle. She is constitutionally lacking the warmth and sensitivity required for the care of a needy child. I knew that and made a point of keeping in touch over the years. So I guess you could say that Alice sees me as the likeliest person to take over.'

Moral issues aside, ignoring the implication that she and Lionel should have offered practical help for an ex-business partner's orphaned child, Isabella Maria's mind was walking an entirely different path. 'Zoe Rothwell was such a pretty child, as I remember. Such a happy little thing. She and her parents spent that Christmas with us at Wakeham Lodge. You remember, Lionel—you and her father spent most of the time finalising the details about buying him out of the business. Weeks later both her parents were dead, so there must be a mass of money sloshing about. Little Zoe might have turned into a handful but she must be worth a great deal. Surely that's right, Javier?'

'So?' Javier bit back his impatience. 'Zoe will inherit a considerable amount when she reaches twenty-one. In the meantime the money's in trust.' He answered the question, even though it had no relevance to the present situation, only to receive another from the same off-beat direction.

'Is she still pretty? I recall she had the loveliest long pale blonde hair—and such huge golden eyes!'

As he expelled an I-don't-believe-this hiss Javier's dark brows met. What had Zoe's looks got to do with the problem he was faced with? Tips on how to persuade a reluctant teenager to finish her education would have been more to the point! 'How should I know?' he grouched. 'I visit a couple of times a year to make sure things are ticking over as well as can be expected, only to be regaled with tales of temper tantrums, nannies disappearing at the speed of light.'

In those days Zoe had been clingy around him on his visits, he recalled. Still at university himself, he'd found fun things to do with the orphaned scrap, given her a few hours of the type of childish fun not permitted by her starchy grandmother or her ancient housekeeper, both of whom repeatedly spouted the principle that children should be seen but not heard.

Later, when Zoe had been packed off to boarding-school, she'd become sulky, her mouth in a perpetual pout, her hair plaited in a tight braid that fell down her back to her waist.

It must have been almost a year since he'd seen her. Pressure of work had kept him out of England. His frown deepened to a scowl. She'd spent the whole of his two-hour visit staring at him, he recalled, re-membering how oddly uncomfortable she'd made him feel.

'You should marry her. She has her own fortune so she wouldn't be spending yours—which is a huge consideration when one never knows if a woman thinks more of the size of a man's wallet than the extent of his happiness,' Isabella Maria pronounced lightly. 'In two years, when she's eighteen. Provided she has child-bearing hips, of course. What could be more convenient? And if anyone could cure her of her apparent habit of bad behaviour then it would be my handsome, strong-minded son!'

'Dream on, Mama!' His mocking laughter was a

release for his irritation. He could never stay annoyed with his outrageous, adored parent for more than two minutes at a time. And as for the state of Zoe's hips, he had no idea whether they were as wide as a barn door or as narrow as a snake's.

Zoe's heart was beating so rapidly she felt sick. The carriage clock on the mantelpiece ticked the interminably slow waiting minutes. Javier was coming for her! Her head was spinning; her whole body felt out of control.

She shifted restlessly on the upright chair in the window enclosure, staring out over the dull November garden, over the top of the low neatly clipped privet hedge where she would see his car as it turned off the village main street and onto the driveway, her eyes stinging with the effort of not allowing herself the smallest blink in case she missed his arrival.

For the first time in her sixteen and a half years she actually believed in her own guardian angel, something or someone who did care about her, nudge her in the right direction. What else could explain her sudden decision to walk out of school, hitch a lift back here and state she was never going back?

She'd hated that school ever since she'd been sent there at the age of eleven. Surrounded by strangers who hadn't known her from Adam and hadn't wanted to—because by that time Zoe had learned that the only way to dull the pain of not being loved by a single living soul was to act as if she didn't care.

The other sixty-odd pupils were meek little swots

and Zoe soon discovered why. The guiding principle of The Blenchley Private Academy For Girls was strict discipline. Severe punishments were handed out for anyone who stepped out of line, no mitigating circumstances considered.

The threat of punishment meant nothing to Zoe. Whatever the grim-eyed tutors dealt out—for answering back, bad attitude, inattention, whatever—meant next to nothing because it was a pale shadow of the punishment she'd been dealt on the night she'd lost both her loving parents, her home, everything. The only survivor from her happy past had been Misty, her darling Shetland pony, safe in his stable. But Grandmother Alice had flatly refused to allow her to keep him. Misty had been sold.

So she'd loathed Grandmother Alice, too. Truth to tell, when the grandmother she'd seen only rarely had taken her in she'd been scared by the way the old lady had recoiled and pushed her away whenever she'd tried to climb on her knee for a cuddle. Zoe had never before encountered an emotional rebuff or been treated as if she were an inconsiderate nuisance. She hadn't liked being scared so she'd turned that fear and bewilderment into anger, a stubborn refusal to do as she was told, ever.

When she'd woken that morning, just over a week ago, and decided she wouldn't stay at school one moment longer, she'd had no idea how events would unfold. Twenty-four hours ago Grandmother Alice had announced, 'Javier Masters has agreed to take you into his care for the remainder of your minority.' Her thin mouth had pursed. 'I have performed my duty thus far, but am unwilling to continue. My only hope is that Javier can instil some common sense into you and exact at least some good behaviour. He will collect you tomorrow afternoon. Make sure you are packed and ready.'

Since then she'd been in a state bordering on delirium. Her guardian angel had been working overtime! She'd always adored Javier.

In the beginning he had given her treats every time he'd visited. Trips to the zoo, ice creams and burgers, a day at the seaside where they'd built the biggest sandcastle known to mankind, a magical few hours watching a pantomime, lots of fun but, more importantly, his time and attention. All that had more or less stopped once she'd been packed away to boarding-school. He'd still visited a couple of times a year when she'd been back on holiday but Grandmother Alice had vetoed any outings, telling Javier that, because of consistently bad reports from school, treats of any kind were out of the question.

The visits she'd so much looked forward to had become torture. The three of them taking tea, served by the grumpy old housekeeper, Grandmother Alice's strictures to 'Sit up straight', 'Don't fidget so', 'Answer the question.'

Javier's gentle questions about school, the friends she'd made, nothing she'd wanted to answer because nobody must know how unhappy she was. It would have made her seem weak and she wasn't, she was tough!

But his smile had always been kind even though she'd known she was behaving like a sulky brat. And when he'd left he'd always given her a big hug and that had always made her want to cry because he'd seemed the only person in the world able to like her, and she'd known it would be months before she would see him again.

Then, around a year ago, on his last visit, something amazing had happened. She'd fallen for him with a resounding crash. Not only because of his fantastic looks—that soft black hair, sexy, black-fringed smoky eyes, the hard slash of his high cheekbones, tough jawline and wide, beautiful male mouth—but because of that intrinsic kindness, coupled with the aura of supreme self-assurance that told her that he was a man who would fight to the death for anything or anyone he cared about.

Flooded with new and heady sensations, butterflies in her tummy, a melting, softening feeling that had sprung from her rapidly beating heart and flooded through every inch of her body, a strange, awe-struck breathlessness, she hadn't been able to take her eyes off him, following every move he'd made, soaking in every word he'd said.

The wonder of falling in love had armoured her against Grandmother Alice's coldness and her return to school at the start of the new year had been accepted blithely. She'd even got her head down and worked hard, toed the line. If she could go home with a good report then her grandmother would have no grounds to veto any outing he might suggest.

She'd felt as if she were floating on a rosy cloud, counting off the days until his next visit, hopefully during the Easter holidays, but if not then definitely some time during the summer. She'd known there wasn't an earthly chance of him falling in love with her—the very idea was insane—but that hadn't stopped her fantasising, or stopped her longing for his next visit.

But it hadn't happened and she'd faced the fact that he had better things to do with his time than check up on her. Why should he? She was no longer a child whose welfare was of some concern to him; she was nearly adult and could look out for herself.

Guessing that she would probably never see him again, experience the luxury of feasting her eyes on him, see him smile for her, receive his goodbye hug had hurt so much she couldn't bear it. So she'd smartly convinced herself that she didn't care. And if she didn't care and no one cared about her then she could go ahead and do her own thing, be whatever she wanted to be.

But Grandmother Alice's news had changed all that, shattered the spiky carapace of indifference she'd built around her heart—a relatively easy exercise since she'd been forced to manage it somehow after the death of her parents.

How much longer would he be?

Restlessness drove her from her chair. From information tartly given she knew he'd flown in from Spain yesterday, had intended to spend the night at his London apartment, get through some business, then drive here to Berkshire. What was taking him so long? She couldn't wait to see him again, be with him. The thought of being in his care for the next two years made her knees go weak.

She grabbed for the heavy velvet curtains to steady herself, her heart racing giddily just as her grandmother entered the room. A small bird-like figure, stiffly postured in her usual black, her face set in the customary lines of long-suffering displeasure, she said sharply, 'If you won't change out of those dreadful things you've taken to wearing then be good enough to cover yourself up with a decent coat. And put a scarf on your head. Javier Masters will take one look at you and wash his hands of you altogether.'

Bristling at the criticism, Zoe swept out of the room, across the black and white paved hall, banging the front door behind her.

When she'd walked out of school she'd vowed never to wear the despised uniform again, or the dreary skirts and cardigans Grandmother Alice ordered from a fuddy-duddy mail-order catalogue whose only customers, Zoe was sure, were housebound ninety-year-olds.

The monthly allowance paid by the trustees was fairly generous and she'd had little opportunity to spend it. It had mounted up. So, her defiance of stultifying authority had reached new heights one day last week when she'd taken the bus to town and spent the lot. Forbidden make-up, hair dye, lots and lots of cheap and cheerful clothes.

Trying on stuff in the communal changing room of the town's trendiest store, she'd felt part of the young happy-go-lucky scene for the first time in her life. Really cool. It had been a great feeling.

Grandmother Alice belonged firmly in the

Victorian era, she told herself as she settled herself on the front step to wait.

Javier was later than he'd expected. Apart from a couple of urgent business calls he'd found that making arrangements for the care of a teenage girl was more daunting than he'd expected it to be.

The picture-perfect Queen Anne house stood back from the village street. He indicated and turned the Jaguar into the drive and stamped on the brakes as a blur of violent colour exploded from the front step.

Zoe?

His startled gaze took in the wild transformation. Gone were the heavy grey tweed skirts and shapeless twinsets, replaced by black leather boots with six-inch heels, a frilled scarlet miniskirt with a weird asymmetric hem, a lacy gypsy top in vivid orange—and what in heaven's name had she done to her hair?

It was bright red, looking as if it had been hacked off by a drunk wielding a pair of garden shears, gelled into tortuous spikes!

His movements slow, he unclasped his seat belt and turned off the ignition. Seeing the way she'd chosen to dress, Alice would have thrown a fit, and he didn't blame her. Had this, coupled with her rebellious granddaughter walking out of school, been the straw that broke the unwilling camel's back?

She was hopping from one booted foot to the other, her skinny arms clasped around her naked midriff. She had to be freezing. Venting a heavy sigh at what he appeared to be taking on, he swung out of the car and straightened his butter-soft charcoal leather jacket. He had accepted the responsibility of guiding Zoe Rothwell through the next two years and he never went back on his word.

As he approached over the immaculate length of the brick-paved drive a huge grin split Zoe's inexpertly cosmetically enhanced features. She's just a kid, a needy kid, he told himself, the warmth of his answering smile instinctive. All teenagers experimented, trying to find out who they were, and he had to be thankful she'd chosen wacky clothes and a violent hairstyle rather than drugs or alcohol! Knowing Alice, he guessed she would have subjected Zoe to tirades of horror and the sort of cold ridicule that would have shattered the girl's confidence. Best keep his mouth shut right now and introduce the subject gently at a later date.

But his good intentions crumpled when he got close enough to see the butterfly tattoo on her left cheekbone. His black brows drawn into a frown, he touched the offending insect with the tip of a long finger.

'Did you have to permanently disfigure yourself?'

She had, he noted abstractedly, an exquisitely pretty face beneath that heavy make-up, and her huge golden eyes danced with amusement. Suddenly, Javier's lungs felt strangely constricted. He stepped back a pace.

'It's a transfer, silly! Don't you know anything?' she came back pertly as soon as she'd found her breath. Heat throbbed the spot he'd touched and spread through her entire body. Her skin might be covered with goose-bumps but she was glowing inside. Life with this gorgeous man was going to be just wonderful! He hadn't made scathing comments about her cool new clothes or thrown a fit when her wild hairstyle had hit him in the eye. With him, away from the rigid discipline doled out by her grandmother and her teachers, she would be able to be herself and do exactly as she pleased for once. She'd always known Javier was the greatest, even when she was a small kid, he'd come through for her, and now he'd rescued her. She had never loved him more!

Half an hour into the journey to Gloucestershire Javier's mouth was getting grimmer. Zoe's parting from her grandmother had wrenched at his heart. The elderly lady couldn't have made it plainer that she was glad to wash her hands of the poor kid. But the perfume she'd obviously drenched herself in was really getting to him. He'd open all the car windows to get rid of the overpowering smell but she'd freeze to death. She'd dropped the school gaberdine the ancient housekeeper had handed her and flounced out to the car, her silly skirt swinging, showing an inordinate amount of smooth thigh, tottering on those wicked spiky heels.

And he'd stopped listening to her prattles of gratitude. From what he could gather she believed she was in for the time of her life. And he'd stopped glancing at her. That lace top thing she was wearing ought to be X-rated. And she wasn't wearing a damn thing underneath. A mixture of anger and concern impacted on his hard features. He could understand why Zoe had so wholeheartedly rebelled against the dreary school uniform and dowdy garments her grandmother had insisted she wear. But she'd gone too far the other way. She might think she looked cool and cutting edge, but in everyone else's eyes she looked tarty.

Time to spell out a few ground rules, show her he had the upper hand and meant business.

'There are a couple of things you ought to know before you get too hooked on the idea that your time with me is going to be a bed of roses. Firstly, I contacted your trustees to put them in the picture about the change of guardianship, only to hear that you've been pestering them to release large sums of money. It's not going to happen, Zoe, so it has to stop. You need anything, you tell me, and if it's reasonable I'll approach the trustees. Understood?'

Reddening at the memory of the response to her request, Zoe shot Javier a fulminating sideways look. 'I don't want a single thing—that was the point. I made a sensible request and got treated like a silly child!' she bristled.

Javier's hands relaxed slightly on the steering wheel. She sounded about ten years old! 'So run the sensible request by me,' he invited lightly.

Zoe's painted mouth twisted with suspicion. Was her darling Javier patronising her? Was she about to get more outright derisive rejection of her ideas? Probably. But knowing that Javier was the one person in the world who could criticise her without getting his head bitten off had her pronouncing with prickly defensiveness, 'There's a load of money in my name doing nothing. And there are loads of people sleeping in doorways or cardboard boxes, people with no one to care about them. The only difference between them and me is I've got a bed to sleep in and obscene amounts of money. I wanted to spread it around to do some good.' She shot him a 'so there!' look and scrunched herself back against the leather seat, waiting for a lecture entitled Immature Profligacy.

'There's a third difference between you and the homeless, Zoe,' Javier said, sympathy for the poor scrap softening his voice. 'You do have people who care about you. Your grandmother for starters. She may not be much good at showing it, but if she didn't care she wouldn't have tried so hard to mould you to her idea of what a young lady should be. She's simply a throwback to the beginning of the last century.'

Ignoring her snort of disbelief, he swung into the appropriate lane for the exit to Cirencester and said firmly, 'And I care. If I didn't I'd have told Alice to take a running jump when she suggested handing you over to me. And getting back to your commendable concern for the homeless, there are better ways of helping than throwing handfuls of cash at every street beggar. If you're still of the same mind when you come into your inheritance we'll discuss it further. Agreed?'

Zoe simply nodded. She couldn't speak without giving herself away. Tears blurred her eyes and clogged her throat. Javier had said he cared about her. He was the only person in the world who could touch her so deeply she wanted to cry!

But her bout of sentimentality took a nosedive when he announced, 'And because I care about your future I insist you finish your education.'

Waiting at traffic lights he glanced across at her. Mutiny writ large on her expressive features, she said on a note of triumph, 'I ran away. They won't take me back!'

'You're enrolled in a sixth-form college in Gloucester. Joe Ramsay will drive you in and collect you daily. You may remember Mrs Ramsay, my housekeeper? Joe's her husband and looks after the grounds. Mrs Ramsay will look after you when I'm not at the lodge.'

Of course she remembered Ethel Ramsay. She had let her help make the mince pies. She remembered everything about the last happy Christmas with her parents, but rarely looked back because it still hurt too much and made her feel weepy when she wanted to be tough.

'And another thing.' Javier hardened his heart. Someone had to tell her she looked like the trollop she wasn't. 'The way you're dressed gives the wrong impression.' How to get the message through without making her feel cheap? 'Besides, it doesn't do you justice. You're a pretty kid and, as I recall, your hair was beautiful.'

Discounting the iffy 'kid' bit, 'Pretty and Beautiful' were like manna from heaven. She shot him a wide-eyed look.

'And?' she asked, scarcely daring to breathe, wondering if his caring was beginning to get a bit more personal.

'You wash that ghastly colour out and let it grow again, and you and I will go shopping for clothes that strike a happy medium between someone's ancient aunt and a slapper. Do we have a bargain?'

It wasn't nearly as personal as she'd have liked,

nothing like a declaration that he fancied her. As if! But it was all a darn sight better than being stuck with Grandmother Alice. And who knew? Living with each other for the next year and a half or so—and maybe even longer, until she was twenty-one, say— he might come to look on her as a young woman instead of a kid. And she'd do anything he asked of her but she wasn't going to let him know that. So. 'Let me get this straight. I go back to school.' A theatrical groan. 'You dictate how I look instead of Grandmother Alice. What's in it for me?'

Javier smothered a grin. He could recognise manipulation when he saw it. The poor kid would have had a miserable eight years with Alice Rothwell and wasn't about to agree to more of the same. 'You do as I want and in term breaks you get grown-up treats. Winter skiing, holidays in Spain. Paris, maybe— whatever you fancy. A deal?'

Happiness threatened to choke her. All that—with him! Heaven had arrived on earth!

'Done!'

CHAPTER ONE

Two and a half years later...

'I'M EVER so sorry for bothering you, Mr Masters,'
Ethel Ramsay ventured as Javier slammed the car
door behind him with force and strode over the gravel
to where she had the main door of Wakeham Lodge
open. With a quiver of apprehension the housekeeper
noted the tension in his wide mouth, the rigid set of
his shoulders beneath the white cotton shirt he wore.

Smouldering with anger, that was what he was,
anyone could see that! And she could understand it
because making sure the construction empire that
straddled the world ran on oiled wheels kept him flat
out, so he wouldn't exactly thank her for dragging
him back here, but she'd been so concerned, so had
Joe—

'You did exactly right, Ethel,' Javier said, making
a conscious effort to keep his tone moderate in view
of the trepidation in her mild brown eyes. 'If anyone
should apologise it is I. I should have kept a closer
eye on things.'

His fault entirely. He'd kept actual face-to-face
contact with Zoe to a minimum for the last fourteen
months, ever since that episode beside the swimming
pool behind his parents' winter home in Southern
Andalucia. He'd thought it best. He now feared he'd

been wrong. His lack of judgement in this case made him furious with himself.

'So where is she?' he questioned as something that looked like a cross between a small hairy hearthrug and a jack-in-the-box shot between his straddled legs and out onto the drive, where it sat, panting in the hot June sun, its head tipped expectantly. 'What the hell is that?'

'Boysie.' Ethel relaxed a little. It would seem that the letter she'd written wasn't responsible for that obvious annoyance, and she felt easier already. Her employer rarely lost his temper but when he did it was spectacular. She hadn't wanted to bring his wrath down on her own head.

She gave a resigned shrug but her eyes smiled as they rested on the small dog. 'Miss Zoe's stray. They're devoted to each other. He'd been wandering the village street for days so she took him in. He leaves hairs all over, I'm afraid, but we have rid him of fleas.'

Javier vented a sigh. So the menagerie had increased by one very ugly dog. At the last count she'd collected three cats from the local rescue centre and an abandoned fox cub, now thankfully half grown, fit and healthy and released back into the wild.

Emotionally starved for most of her formative years, Zoe needed something to love, so her menagerie was fine by him. At least he was no longer the recipient—

'Where is she now?' He repeated his query, walking further into the coolness of the wide hallway.

'On a driving lesson.' Ethel's kindly face puckered

with a concern Javier didn't then understand. A few weeks ago Zoe had phoned him with the perfectly reasonable request that she have her own car. After all, she was pushing nineteen. The trustees had agreed and had coughed up. So a driving lesson gave him no problems and allowed him more time to delve deeper into his housekeeper's worrying written request, faxed through to him on a construction site in northern France by his senior PA. 'You are needed here,' it had informed him. 'Miss Zoe's got mixed up with a wild crowd. Me and Joe do our best but it isn't enough.'

He needed to know far more before he confronted Zoe.

'Then you've time to paint a clearer picture.' One hand cupping her plump elbow, he drew her into the sunlit drawing room, where she refused to sit, just stated with breathy agitation, 'The driving's part of the bigger problem. She—Miss Zoe, bless her, insisted on buying one of those flashy sports cars. Joe tried to persuade her to go for something more suited to a learner but she wouldn't listen, she'd rather listen to the likes of that Oliver Sherman. And do you know what? He somehow persuaded her to let him keep the car, and he comes up here in it most afternoons to take her out supposedly to teach her to drive, and he's already smashed up two of his own cars to my certain knowledge! And that's not the worst of it.' Her face was getting steadily redder. 'She's taken up with a fast crowd, at least they took up with her—mostly for what they can get out of her, is what me and Joe reckon. You'll know, of course, how her allowance

got a hefty lift upwards after she turned eighteen—
well, it goes on that crowd of hangers-on and that
Sherman is the worst of them. Always hanging
around her. I've tried to warn her, so has Joe, but she
takes not a bit of notice. She stays out all hours. I've
caught her coming in at dawn often enough. And another thing—'

Her catalogue of woes was cut short by the sound
of an engine at speed, the squeal of brakes and the
showering of gravel. 'That will be them—'

His mouth set in a hard, flat line, Javier strode out
with long, impatient steps. The bright yellow Lotus
was parked alongside his Jag and even through the
windscreen he could see that Zoe looked shaken. His
mouth took on a grimmer line.

Ignoring her for the moment—he'd deal with her
later—he wrenched open the driver's side door and
removed the ignition keys.

'Out!' The single word exploded with cutting ar-
rogance.

The initial look of utter shock was replaced by
sulky belligerence on Oliver Sherman's playboy-
pretty features. 'And what if I won't?' he muttered.

'I didn't hear that,' Javier gritted. What he knew
of Sherman, spoiled only child of a local estate agent
with a decidedly dubious reputation, put him firmly
in the low-life category. He didn't want him anywhere
near Zoe. 'You've two seconds to get out under your
own steam.' His voice carried a steely threat that the
younger, shorter man wisely chose not to ignore.

'Start walking.'

'But—' An ugly tide of red swept over the blond's

face, his pale blue eyes swivelling over the roof of the car to where Zoe was standing, a wriggling, face-licking Boysie high in her arms. As if his courage had been bolstered by that moment of eye contact, he drawled, 'Zoe allows me use of her car; it's not for you to say.'

'No?'

Unwavering grey eyes turned to black ice. Shrivelled, Oliver Sherman took a shaky backwards step, turned, and began to walk.

For a moment or two, Zoe watched his retreat with a surge of relief. Ollie hadn't let her behind the wheel at all today, claiming he had better things to do than sit beside a learner who didn't know her clutch from her windscreen washer.

He'd driven them up onto Kenley Common and tried it on. She was used to his passes, his protestations of love and marriage proposals and could handle them one hand tied behind her back, no problem.

But today he'd got really heavy and she'd literally had to fight him off, and that wasn't her idea of harmless fun. And coming back he'd driven like a maniac, which hadn't been a bundle of laughs, either.

Happily, she dismissed him from her mind. She was supposed to be seeing him tonight with some of the others, and no doubt he would try to make a joke out of her guardian's old-fashioned heavy-handedness and if she defended him, as she knew she would, they would think she was really uncool. Besides, she didn't want to go clubbing while Javier was here. So she'd cancel.

She turned her attention to Javier, a river of delicious excitement running right through her. He was still watching Ollie tramp down the long drive. The moment she'd seen him walk out to the car, his face like a thundercloud, her heart had soared on wings of joy. He'd been away for so long. She'd missed him for every minute of every day. Giving Boysie one last cuddle, she set the little dog down on its small hairy feet and walked round the bonnet of her gorgeous little car towards him.

Dancing eyes watched the way he slid her car keys into the pocket of the sleek-fitting dark trousers of a business suit, watched the play of seriously honed shoulder muscles beneath the fine white cotton of his shirt as he at last turned to face her.

'You came! You remembered!' She could hardly get the words out through a smile wide enough to split her face in two, through the absence of breath that always afflicted her when in his presence.

He said nothing, just studied her through the thick veiling of those heavy black lashes, his beautiful all-male features impassive. 'Remembered?' he enquired blankly.

So he hadn't come to celebrate her birthday with her tomorrow. Her smile slipped then powered out again. It didn't matter. He was here, that was all that mattered. She desperately wanted to hurl herself at him and give him a huge hug of welcome but knew she mustn't. After what had happened in Spain he would think she was making amorous advances again. Her cheeks reddened at the embarrassing memory of how crass and obvious she'd been.

Belatedly, she answered his question with a tiny

dismissive shrug. 'Nothing. Forget it.' This time her smile was simply polite. She must make herself remember not to wear her heart on her sleeve. 'It's lovely to see you. How long are you staying?' If he said five minutes she'd curl up and die with disappointment!

He gave her a level look as inner anger stirred. He should have kept a closer watch over her, dammit. A flash of memory seared his brain. The only holiday he'd shared with her. At his parents' winter home near Almeria. Zoe scrambling out of the pool as he approached. Her tiny bikini. Throwing herself at him, arms clinging, lips kissing, lips saying 'I love you, love you! I always have!'

His put-down had been firm but kind. Surely he'd been kind? Whatever, the incident had thrown him off balance, making him neglect a duty for the first time in his adult life. He'd kept physically well away from her, knowing that the schoolgirl crush would fade to nothing but an embarrassing memory if it had nothing to feed on.

He vented an impatient breath. He was wasting time. He wasn't here to beat himself up over past mistakes. He gave back, 'Long enough to sort out your immediate future. Shall we go in?'

Tensing, trying not to let her draining disappointment show, Zoe followed, the faithful Boysie at her heels. He hadn't been able to hide that flash of anger, or keep the impatience from his voice. Was he still mad at her for not trying to find a place at university as he and the trustees had suggested?

Or was he just plain fed up with having his self-inflicted care of her hanging around his neck like a heavy weight he wanted rid of? Regretting ever having agreed to Grandmother Alice's request?

It surely looked like it, Zoe thought numbly as she followed him into the spacious sitting room. The early loss of both her parents coupled with Grandmother Alice's emotional rejection had taught her not to let anyone get close enough to hurt her.

Except for Javier.

Why did she still love him, want him as close to her as a second skin? Why lay herself open to the desperate hurt he'd been unknowingly doling out ever since they'd made that bargain on the day he'd driven her away from her grandmother's home?

She prided herself on being a tough cookie—was she tough enough to accept that he'd never see her as anything but a bit of a nuisance, the rare claims she made on his attention a waste of his precious time? Time he'd much prefer to be spending on his business empire or the latest sophisticated, full-grown woman to be sharing his bed.

She'd have to be, wouldn't she? Starting as of now! Ignoring the sweep of a strong, long-fingered hand towards one of the armchairs that flanked the flower-filled hearth, she walked to the padded window-seat, clutched at Boysie as he leapt onto her lap and turned her cool golden gaze on Javier.

He didn't sit. He felt too wired up. Zoe Rothwell had developed into quite something since he'd last seen her. The pale, water-straight blonde hair had grown, framing delicately lovely features, her skin smooth and warmed by a light summer tan. A tall girl, five eight at a guess, her body was supple as a sapling, the pale cream cotton trousers she was wearing emphasising the graceful length of her legs, the narrowness of her waist where the sleeveless button-through tawny top she was wearing tucked into the waistband.

He could quite see why Sherman was sniffing around her—and with her future fortune as a welcome bonus he wouldn't give up all that easily! The unwanted memory of how her practically naked body had felt against his assaulted his brain. He had done the right and honourable thing but that low-life would have taken full advantage. His fists clenched at his side, the knuckles showing white against the taut, tanned skin.

But before he waded in, all guns blazing, he had to find out just what her relationship with Sherman was, quiz her about the wild crowd Ethel had mentioned. For all he knew his housekeeper might be overreacting. Bunching his fists into the pockets of his trousers, he frowningly sought the right opening, but his mind kept straying to the way the sunlight through the window behind her gilded her pale hair, wondering if it felt as silky as it looked. His frown deepened. He hated this unprecedented inability to concentrate on the matter in hand.

Judging by the scowl that brought those black brows down above the narrowed, silver-glinting beautiful eyes, Javier was wishing he'd never set eyes on her. A wash of desperate emptiness drained the light out of her eyes. Almost four years ago she'd fallen in love with him and since then he'd rarely been out of her mind.

Long years of wondering when he'd visit, of waiting for the post in case he'd written, of her heart jumping into her mouth every time the phone rang, longing for it to be Javier asking to speak to her, of trying to model herself on the type of women he favoured, sleek, sophisticated and sexy. And a fat lot of good that had done her when he hadn't clapped eyes on her for over a year!

She'd behaved like a spineless lovesick wimp. And it had to stop. Right now. He'd never feel anything for her other than irritation if his present taut, straddle-legged stance and frowning charcoal gaze was anything to go by. So what? she asked herself on a spurt of self-protective rebellion. So she should get herself a life and not mourn what she could never have.

In the tense silence she registered the inward tug of his breath, saw the firm mouth begin to relax and jumped in before he could give her a lecture, most probably about her unsuitable choice of car. The last thing she wanted to do was quarrel with him. She had to stay cool if her newborn resolve to put what she felt for him behind her and make a life for herself was to stand any chance at all of surviving.

'You said you wanted to discuss my immediate future.'

'Exactly.' His eyes narrowed on the way her slender fingers were fondling the ugly dog's floppy ears. The weird little creature looked as if it were in paradise.

Her chin lifted at a proud angle, defiance in her eyes as she gave him her steady regard. 'I've decided it's time to split,' she told him levelly. 'I'm legally adult. I've kept my side of the bargain we made and you've kept yours—to the letter, if not the spirit. So—'

'Whoa!' Javier put in, suddenly intrigued by the clipped concisiveness of her cool silver voice, the implied criticism. 'Are you telling me I've gone back on any of the promises I made?'

'No, of course not.' Zoe averted her eyes from his too-fabulous lean features. Drinking in the hard slash of his cheekbones, the mind-blowing masculine sensuality of that kissable mouth was definitely no part of the cure she was utterly determined to effect.

'I finished my education in exchange for the holiday treats you dangled under my nose,' she pointed out with perfect cool. 'You arranged the promised skiing break—and sent your current woman with me. Glenda, wasn't it? Did you really have to bribe her, as she told me you did? Then there was Paris—Sophie went with me. And we mustn't forget the Italian lakes—Sophie again, or—'

'Enough.' A raised hand sliced her to silence, which, she belatedly realised was just as well because he wasn't a fool and he'd be getting the message that the term break treats had meant nothing to her without him. Besides, the only time he'd accompanied her, the Easter before last, had led to that shamefully revealing episode beside his parents' swimming pool and that was something she was determined to forget about. Pretend it hadn't happened.

'I wanted you to have some fun in your life,' he told her solemnly. 'I cared about you, but I'm not cut out for hands-on nannying,' he qualified.

'Cared about'. Past tense. That said it all, didn't it just. She'd been a brat and for some reason he'd felt sorry for her and taken her under his wing. But now she was adult he wanted rid of the responsibility. Even though it was something she'd suspected, hearing it put into words hurt so much. She felt like bursting into tears of heartbreak. But wouldn't let herself. She had to handle this like the adult she was. Make a clean break. Forget him. Make her own life.

'Exactly.' Her voice was cool but she felt sick inside. 'I no longer need nannying so consider yourself off the hook. I intend to ask the trustees to let me buy a small place of my own. I want my independence.'

Javier's mouth flattened with irritation. 'Independence to do what? Run around with the likes of Sherman, stay out all night with no one to ask awkward questions, get behind the wheel of a racy sports car you haven't the experience to handle?' Not while he had breath in his body!

Zoe compressed her full lips, her eyes sparking rebellion. Ethel had been telling tales. That was what his rare appearance was all about! Nothing to do with wanting to say hello, spend some time with her.

'A girl needs to have some fun,' she sliced at him, affecting a blaséness she was far from feeling. She'd been lonely here so she'd done something about it. Joined the local tennis club, made friends, mixed with a smooth crowd, blowing her allowance on new clothes, treating her mates to lavish meals at fancy restaurants, clubbing, champagne flowing. She knew her friends sucked up to her for what they could get out of her but she didn't care. At least their flattery and company helped fill the empty space in her life. Ollie might say he loved her, but she knew he didn't. The only unconditional love she had came from Boysie and her cats.

As if to demonstrate her spiky inner thoughts a sleek black cat jumped through the open window behind her and with a chirrup of pleasure settled high on her chest, much to Boysie's annoyance.

Javier's dark brows met as compassion flooded his veins. She'd said a girl needed fun but what this girl needed was love. She'd been starved of it since she was eight years old and that had made her tricky. Tricky and needy, easy prey for the likes of Sherman. It was up to him to keep her safe. There was no one else.

Venting a sigh, he joined her on the window-seat and took the hairy little dog onto his own lap. The black cat settled more comfortably on Zoe's knee. She was stroking it, her hair falling forward, veiling her face from him. His eyes were strangely mesmerised by the movements of those long, slender fingers.

Gathering himself, he pointed out flatly, 'You have to know that I'd veto any suggestion that you have your own place at the moment, but that doesn't mean we have to fight over it.'

No verbal reaction. Just a slight stiffening of her slender shoulders. He resisted the strong urge to pull her towards him, give her a reassuring cuddle. It would ease his conscience but, recalling the incident in Spain, she might get the wrong idea.

'What I suggest is this—we book you a crash course of professional driving lessons and keep the Lotus locked in a garage until you're capable of handling it. And we'll decide what you want to do with your life. I'll make sure I'm around to help you,' he impressed heavily, continuing more lightly, 'You once said you were interested in charity work; that might be the way to go. On the other hand,' he ploughed on—difficult to keep sounding like a kindly uncle in the face of her total lack of response—'you could enrol for a course in anything that takes your fancy.'

Setting the cat down, Zoe got to her feet, her movements fluidly dismissive. Wordlessly, she left the room, her golden head high. The little dog leapt from Javier's lap and pattered after her. Javier's chest tightened with an inward tug of breath. Guilt swamped him. He blamed himself for her wayward non-cooperation; he should have been around far more often. When she'd been a kid he'd known how to handle her, she'd always responded to him. He didn't know what made the newly adult woman tick.

Zoe hadn't let herself cry. She never cried. But the hurt was difficult to push away. As little as an hour ago she would have welcomed his interference in her life with open arms if it meant he was going to be around more often. Bent over backwards to please him, knowing he would be giving her his time and attention, clinging onto the childish hope that he would grow to feel something for her.

But that wasn't going to happen. She had finally accepted it. At long last she had stopped fantasising.

When Oliver Sherman rang her mobile she sat cross-legged on her bedroom carpet to take his call. His run-in with Javier hadn't fazed him. Merely, 'Your guardian's a bossy bastard, Zo, but it needn't spoil our plans. Obviously, I can't pick you up this evening, but Guy's willing. He's bringing Jenny, and the three of us will collect you at seven—I thought we'd eat first so I booked us in at Anton's for half past and we'll go on from there. OK? Oh, and while I think about it, you can give me the keys and I'll pick the Lotus up when we bring you back, provided the boss is tucked up in bed! I hate being without wheels and until I hear from the insurance bods about my latest write-off, I'm stuck. You still there, Zo?'

She pulled in a deep breath. Because Javier was home she'd fully intended to cancel. But things had changed. Her determination to stop herself loving him was still a touch shaky so it would be better if she didn't have to spend too much time around him.

A fun evening with her friends, even if she did end up picking up the tab, was probably just what she needed to take her mind off Javier. And she'd grab the opportunity to take Ollie aside and tell him that if he wanted to keep her friendship and have the loan of her car in return for teaching her to drive, there must be no more repetitions of what had happened this afternoon.

'Seven it is, then,' she said coolly and cut the connection.

Zoe was on the doorstep at five to. All trigged out in her finest, making a statement.

Her freshly washed hair was caught back from one side of her face with a sparkling gold clip, echoing the gold of the band she wore on one wrist, picking up the tawny bronze of her sleeveless, almost backless silk sheath, the finishing touch of strappy bronze sandals adding four inches to her height.

Her mirror had told her she looked flirty. Expensive and flirty, startlingly reminiscent of the Glendas and Sophies of unfond memory. Set for a fun evening with smooth friends who knew their way around. Which should show Javier that he couldn't interfere in her life.

Even Ethel, catching sight of her as she'd sauntered down the stairs, had popped her eyes. 'I take it you won't be in for dinner?'

'Full marks for observation,' had been her less than friendly response, pay-back time for snitching on her, a response she had immediately regretted because she liked Ethel in spite of her habit of handing out boring lectures. She would apologise tomorrow, she vowed as Ethel turned on the heels of her sensible shoes and bustled away. She wouldn't want to hurt her for the world.

And quite why she'd been in such a sudden rush was made clear when moments later Javier appeared at her side.

The inside of his head felt hot and churned. She looked stunning. The thought of her out on the loose made his brain boil.

'Going somewhere?' he gritted, his eyes sliding with involuntary precision down the length of her exquisite naked spine, dragging them smartly away as she dipped her head in acknowledgement, adding, not looking at him, 'With my friends,' laying cool emphasis on the final word.

'Including Sherman?'

'Naturally.' Zoe didn't have the courage to look at him. He was so close. Everything inside her seemed to leap out, strain to touch him. Her body was needy for him, for the strong warmth of his arms, the touch of his beautifully made hands, for his mouth, his wanting mouth...

She was getting nowhere in her useless attempt to stop loving him! Still fantasising about how his mouth would feel if he kissed her! Her teeth gritted together, her shoulders tensing as she willed Guy's car to appear on the long sweeping drive so that she could jump in and escape.

As her ears strained for the sound of an engine Javier's words came like an electric shock. 'Go to the study. Now,' he added with deadly purpose as he watched her head jerk up and back in what he knew had to be defiance. Tacking on with grim determination, 'Go under your own steam or I carry you. It's your choice. I'll let Sherman know you won't be available to see him.'

Which was no choice at all, Zoe acknowledged on an inner flutter of dread mixed up with a treacherous vein of excitement. Javier didn't make idle threats; he always meant what he said. Her mouth went dry. If she didn't do exactly as he'd told her to he would scoop her into his arms and carry her. If he touched her she wouldn't stand a chance. She would go up in flames of delirium.

She turned on her spiky heels and walked back through the house and heard the sound of Guy's engine. So much for a wild evening out, the prospect of getting Javier out of her head for a few hours.

The prospect of getting him out of her heart would take more than that, she acknowledged glumly. She'd been a fool to think it could be easily accomplished. And now, she supposed, she was in for another lecture!

Zoe was standing in front of one of the tall study windows that overlooked the garden. She turned slowly at his approach, tall, graceful and stunningly lovely. Something tightened around his heart. The golden eyes, so like the topaz ear droppers he'd picked out while passing through London this morning to mark her birthday tomorrow, might be flashing defiance but there was an aching vulnerability about her soft mouth that sent rivers of sweetly sharp compassion flowing through his veins.

He tugged in a deep, shuddering breath and crossed to the drinks cabinet. He took his time over selecting a bottle of red wine, opening it, pouring it into two glasses. Laying down the law over the lack of structure in her present lifestyle would get him nowhere. Her grandmother and the teachers at her boarding-school had tried harsh discipline, resulting not in the desired meek compliance but in open defiance.

Zoe wouldn't be pushed, but she could be led.

Trouble was, she was no longer a child, a fact brought home as he turned, a glass in each hand, his eyes veiled as he watched her sink into a chair, her long, elegant legs displayed as the narrow skirt of her dress rode up to well above her shapely knees.

A loose cannon was his immediate and uncomfortable thought.

Slender fingers closed round the stem of the glass he offered, one delicate brow rose as she drawled, 'Wine. How liberal of you. I'd rather expected a can of fizzy pop or a beaker of milk.'

Javier acknowledged the dig with a grim smile. Maybe he had been guilty of treating her like a kid—he'd been guilty of too many things where she was concerned. Time to make amends.

Pale blonde tendrils of hair curved around the slender line of her throat. He could see a pulse beating just above the fabric of her dress where it flowed down to skim the outline of perfectly rounded, unfettered breasts.

His throat tightening, Javier stalked over to the desk, leaned against it, half sitting, facing the glorious creature who was like a bomb primed to go off at any moment. With her stunning looks, her need for the love that had been denied her, she would be easy prey for a man on the make. A man like Oliver Sherman.

And she was his responsibility. A strange idea was forming at the back of his mind. He thrust it aside. Time to get the ball rolling.

'Picking up on our earlier conversation, what do

you intend to do with your future?' How strangely thick his voice sounded!

Zoe's tummy lurched. She buried her nose in her glass. Despite all her good intentions she hadn't been able to take her eyes off him. Tension emanated from the tight, burning knot low in her pelvis. Her vow to slice him out of the place in her heart he'd occupied for so long was wretchedly feeble in the face of the magnetic power he wielded over every last one of her senses.

Tough talk, a show of indifference to whatever lecture he might be about to hand out, was the only defence she could think of. Counter-productive to allow him to know she'd been already thinking along the lines of working to help the homeless, but didn't know how to go about it.

Confessing that, admitting to inadequacy, would simply ensure he stayed around, driving her mad with wanting him, her sensible decision to stop loving him biting the dust with a vengeance. He would pull out all the stops to set her on the right road, make time for her, choosing the right charity, making sure the trustees agreed to her finding a small flat near her place of work, probably even visiting sometimes, checking up on her, doing what he would see as his duty—

'Don't worry about me.' She essayed a tiny throw-away shrug and put her empty glass down on a handy side table. 'I'm no longer your responsibility, remember. I might even marry Ollie,' she threw in idly. A bare-faced lie—she wouldn't dream of doing any such thing—but it would get Javier off her case. If she were an about-to-be-married woman his self-inflicted duty to her could be crossed off his list of tiresome responsibilities. 'He's asked me often enough.' She levelled a hopefully dismissive look at him. 'I'll send you an invitation.'

Blind rage darkened Javier's eyes, set his shoulders tautening beneath the soft fabric of his shirt. So her relationship with that low-life scum was more serious than he'd hoped. How could he stand by and see her ruin her life by marrying a man who, to his certain knowledge, had never done a day's work in his rotten life, whose reputation locally was lower than a snake's belly! The weird idea jumped back into vision. It wasn't as crazy as he had at first thought.

'You want to be married? Marry me.'

Some impulses were crazy. This was not. He could keep her safe from predatory males.

Silenced by shock, Zoe could only stare, her eyes widening by the second. How many times had her foolish heart driven her to dream up marriage-proposal scenarios? Millions!

At last she managed a strangled, 'You can't be serious!'

'Never more so.'

Something inside her crumpled. It was what she had dreamed of for years. Yet—'You don't even like me,' she accused thickly.

Javier released his breath on an incredulous sigh. Not like her? The Spanish in him brought his proud head high. 'I've cared about you since you were a bereaved eight-year-old transplanted into a cold, unloving environment. I cared enough to take you off your grandmother's hands. I admired your spirit when you dug your heels in and decided to go your own way—even if you had turned yourself into a fright,' he admitted with one of those smiles guaranteed to take her breath away. 'And it is precisely because I care about you that I'm suggesting we marry.'

Dared she translate 'care' into 'love'? Unconsciously Zoe shook her head. But could she stop herself? Her bones tightened. Fine tremors attacked every inch of her tense frame.

Flaring black brows drew together as the episode in Spain came back to taunt him. From her attitude towards him this afternoon, her worrying relationship with Sherman, he was as sure as dammit that she'd outgrown that schoolgirl crush. In any event, it was time to spell out precisely what he had in mind.

'Needless to say, it would be a marriage on paper. I wouldn't expect you to share my bed. Simply my life and my home for the next two years when, with guidance, you'll be able to prioritise your values and decide what you really want to do with your life and how best to manage your future inheritance. Naturally, an annulment would follow,' he impressed gently, concerned for her.

He could see how her slender hands were shaking, even though they were tightly clasped together in an attempt to disguise it. And all the natural colour had ebbed from her face. His voice lowered with soft persuasion. 'In the meantime as my wife you would be protected from the likes of Sherman, men who would marry you for your money, exploit your open, generous nature and make your life a misery. Try to remember, your future inheritance is no secret. Word gets around and brings the low-life out of the woodwork.'

Zoe got to her feet with difficulty. She felt giddy and nauseous with the pain of hearing his proposal, featuring so often in her soppy daydreams, turn into such a nightmare. But she managed, albeit shakily, 'As a proposal of marriage, that sucks!'

She wasn't going to cry. She never cried! But her wretched eyes had other ideas and flooded her face with scalding, humiliating rivers. Scrubbing furiously, she shot at him, 'So by your reckoning no one could love me for me. Only for my money! That makes me—' her voice threatened to disintegrate '—feel—feel really good about myself!'

Her objective was the door. She managed six inches before she was cradled in his arms, the free-flow of her tears soaking his shirt.

For a few short moments Javier held her in self-loathing silence. He hadn't meant to hurt her. The muffled sobs that were shaking her supple frame mortified him. 'Don't cry,' he murmured against the silky top of her head. He had to comfort her. Had to. Her hair smelled of summer flowers. 'Of course you'll be loved for yourself, I promise you. You are beautiful, intelligent and spirited. How could you not be?' he impressed.

No more sobs. Her body had stilled within the circle of his arms. Poor scrap! He patted her shoulder blades, the avuncular intention somehow getting lost as his hands slid down to the narrow span of her waist and lingered there.

'I was clumsy,' he confessed. How soft and warm her skin felt beneath the thin fabric. 'But the thought of you throwing your life away on the likes of Sherman got me on the raw. You deserve better. Much better. I just want to protect you.'

Slowly, Zoe's head came up. She could hardly breathe for the welter of emotions that were making her heart beat as if she'd just run a marathon. When he'd said she was beautiful he had sounded sincere. He must mean it. And he'd been so quick to recognise how hurt she'd been, quick to offer the comfort of his arms. More than comfort. She felt her body stir, the core of her melt; her eyes swept up to mesh with his.

Eyes awash with tears. Glowing and golden, damp, naturally dark lashes tangled. Lush mouth vulnerably parted, very slightly quivering. Was she still hurt, unsure of her own worth? A solitary tear slid down to the corner of her soft lips. He vented an interior savage oath for his earlier crassness just as a wash of tenderness drenched through him. This girl needed kissing…

CHAPTER TWO

ZOE was having a hard time keeping her cool. She wanted to throw her arms in the air, punch holes in the sky, shout and leap all over the place. Sheer joy made her feel as if she were about to explode.

She'd got a silly grin on her face and didn't care who saw it. Her love-drenched, sparkly eyes swept the length of the lodge's wide terrace to where her brand-new husband was keeping a watchful eye on his father as he confidently coped with his walking cane and the broad flight of steps down to the south lawn where the buffet table was ready for the guests.

His six-feet-plus athletic frame was clothed in formal pale grey suiting, his dark hair gleaming in the early July sun. He was so spectacular. Her heart jumped beneath the fitted jacket of her cream silk suit as she lovingly assimilated every line of his impressive profile. Lingering on the perfect blade of his aristocratic nose, then the set of that sensual mouth, the high slashing cheekbones.

Now he was hers!

She blithely discounted the time limit, the hands-off rule he'd put on their marriage. Javier didn't know it yet, poor deluded darling, but she would do all in her power to make him rethink that preposterous scenario!

That kiss had had her changing her mind at the

speed of light about vehemently turning down his hurtful suggestion of a paper marriage. True, he had stepped back, gently put her away from him, but in those blissful, mind-blowing moments when that kiss had turned into something eager, primal and shattering she had felt that strong body harden in raw response and had known, just known, that she could turn their marriage into a proper one, make him happy, give him children.

During the three weeks since she'd accepted his less-than-flattering proposal—with an equally unflattering, 'I might as well marry you, if it will get you off my case for a couple of years'—she'd been sorely tempted to instigate another of those wild and cataclysmic kisses. But with new maturity she knew she had to be patient, play the waiting game, because if he knew how she really felt about him he'd retract it and probably run a mile.

'Come and join your guests, *nuera*. They are few but they expect you, *sí*?' Isabella Maria, wildly elegant in a flowing peacock-blue brocaded silk coat topped by a cartwheel hat, tucked her hand beneath Zoe's elbow. 'I am too happy to know my son has at last taken my advice to marry to complain too much about that quiet civil ceremony or the wedding celebrations that could be mistaken for a wake.'

'I know what you mean.' Zoe swallowed a giggle as she fell in step beside her mother-in-law, her eyes glowing beneath the shallow brim of a cream tulle hat decorated with tiny yellow rosebuds. Seated stiffly at the table, Grandmother Alice and her ancient companion/housekeeper looked like black crows and the

Ramsays, Ethel and Joe, in their Sunday best didn't look much more festive.

'Javier wanted a really low-key wedding,' Zoe confessed cheerfully. 'Just our immediate family and the Ramsays who would have been very hurt to be left out—he's always treated them like equals, not a bit like paid servants.'

'And this is what you wanted?' Isabella Maria had no interest in the Ramsays' standing in her son's household. 'You could have had the wedding of the year, a marquee packed with the great and the good, the cream of society, music and dancing, everyone admiring and envying you.'

Not giving Zoe the chance to explain that she would have married Javier in the back of a dustcart with two tramps hauled up off the street as witnesses if he had so directed, Isabella Maria slowed her steps and lowered her voice, 'A word of advice, *nuera*, in future don't let Javier get all his own way. He is tough when he needs to be and can appear remote. But underneath he has the soft heart. And you, my dear, have emerged into quite a beauty. Use the gifts nature gave you wisely and you will twist him round your smallest finger.'

As Zoe had been thinking along similar lines since the revelation of that steamy, X-rated kiss the advice was unnecessary. But Isabella Maria had thrown in a remark about having given her son advice on the subject of marriage. She was about to ask what pearls of wisdom had been offered, but the words died in her throat as Javier strode to meet them. If he was impatient of their painfully slow progress he didn't show it. The smoky eyes were slightly veiled and his voice was light as he told them, 'The caterers are waiting.'

The smile he shafted in her direction was full of knee-buckling charm, his hard jawline faintly blue-shadowed. Zoe's heart began to race as she firmly quelled the almost imperative need to trace the lines of that devastatingly handsome face with the tips of her fingers.

Instead, she tucked her hand beneath his arm, her fingertips tightening all on their own, seeking his male warmth, the taut male flesh beneath the fine fabric of his jacket. Her body swayed close to his as they descended the terrace steps. Curvy hip against the narrow male equivalent, thigh brushing thigh, creating unbelievable tension. Wild rose colour mounting to her cheeks, Zoe was making no apologies. No one but she and Javier knew this was supposed to be a paper marriage, excluding intimacies. But wouldn't everyone think it highly peculiar if the newly wedded bride and groom avoided each other like the plague?

But his urbanity as he handed her to her place opposite her grandmother couldn't be faulted. Zoe laid her bouquet of pale yellow and cream roses on the pristine white table-top, her heart still crashing around like a wild bird in a cage. Hadn't Javier felt anything of the sexual excitement that had been making her breathless, weak at the knees? He had shown no sign of being similarly affected.

Her spirits took a momentary dip and to comfort herself she reached for the topaz ear droppers he had gifted her on her birthday and reminded herself that it was early days.

As Javier settled his mother opposite his already seated father Alice Rothwell inclined her severely sculpted white head. 'Normally, I would consider a gel of nineteen far too young to marry. But in your case I congratulate you. Javier will make sure you toe the line; you couldn't be in better hands. Already there is a vast improvement since I last saw you.'

Which made Zoe feel like an infant again, but the reference to the day she'd been handed over to Javier, the rebellious make-over, the sight she must have presented to her starchy relative made her want to apologise for the headaches she must have inflicted on everyone around.

But Javier slipping into his seat beside her stilled her tongue. The caterers had been busy filling champagne glasses and he lifted his flute to her. His smile was everything that could be expected of a man toasting his new bride but his eyes were remote as the icy, empty tracts of the South Pole.

A shudder fell down the length of her spine. Had she bitten off more than she could hope to chew? Then, annoyed with the unknown wimpishness that had had her nearly backing off at the sight of the first hurdle, she tucked into the first course of caviare and blinis, her smile at its stunning brightest, instigating a light conversation, making sure the guests joined in.

She had never been short on determination. So maybe she had been negative in its use in the past. Now she would bring the power of it to bear on something truly positive, gaining Javier's respect and, the best prize of all, his love.

Halfway through the chicken in aspic served with

hot crusty rolls and a crisp green salad, a small shaggy whirlwind, complete with a white satin ribbon tied onto his collar in honour of the occasion, leapt onto Zoe's lap, to a dismayed, 'One of the caterers must have let him out! I told them not to!' from Ethel.

'Put the creature down, child. It's not seemly or hygienic,' said Grandmother Alice, with a disapproving glance at Ethel who was struggling to her feet. 'Someone should make sure it's properly tied up.'

One look at the beam of pleasure on his bride's face as she held the squirming bundle of hair, receiving its ecstatic attentions, had Javier insisting, 'Sit down, Ethel. Boysie's my wife's devoted slave, he deserves to share her day.' And to ram home his point he selected a juicy morsel of chicken from his plate and gave it to the rescued stray, received a look of undying doggy devotion and decided that the animal wasn't as ugly as he'd thought it was.

Wiping his fingers on a linen napkin, he took delivery of Zoe's dazzlingly wide smile and found himself returning it with interest. He had done the right thing in putting his ring on her finger. Shown some kindness and understanding, she was malleable as putty—he'd always known that and had tried to act on it when she'd been younger. In the two years ahead of them he would help to motivate her, give her all the guidance and encouragement she needed to carve out a worthwhile future for herself. And her position as his wife would keep the leeches away.

The rest of the wedding breakfast passed in a glorious daze as far as Zoe was concerned. Javier had stood up for her and her pet against Grandmother

Alice but what was even more fantastic was the way he'd called her *my wife*! Hearing those words from his lips made her go gooey inside like warm treacle.

Only when one of the caterers appeared holding a bouquet of scarlet roses and orange lilies as big as a dustbin, to announce that the car had arrived to ferry Mrs Rothwell and her companion home, did Zoe's starry-eyed conviction that having Javier take her side, call her *my wife*, anoint her with that fantastic, knee-buckling smile of his, meant she was halfway to her secret objective take a swift nosedive.

Accepting the enormous bouquet, Zoe placed it on the end of the table, her brow pleating. She had no idea who could have sent it and in her opinion it was completely OTT, borderline vulgar. With Javier attentively at her shoulder she extracted the small oblong envelope, curiosity driving her to read the enclosure.

Then she wished she hadn't. The paper fluttered from her fingers and her face went fiery red. Her heart squeezed painfully as Javier retrieved it and read:

Congrats, Zo, on nabbing a rich sucker! I know you only turned me down due to my lack of the folding stuff. No lack in other departments—don't we both know it! So when the old man bores you, you know where to find me. Ollie.

Crunching the offensive message into a savagely moulded ball, Javier tossed it aside, dealt Zoe a black, unreadable look and smoothly strode off, urbanity itself now to help Grandmother Alice collect her belongings, standing aside as the old lady unbent enough to drop the first kiss she had ever bestowed on Zoe's cheek, then walking the black-clad pair towards the front of the massive house where their car was waiting.

Watching him go, Zoe felt defeat wash over her in heavy black waves. Back to square one, or even further. Javier's opinion of her would be rock-bottom. Miserably she regretted having thrown at him that she might marry Ollie, not having meant a word of it because it had sprung from deep hurt and anger.

If she ever saw Oliver Sherman again she would throttle him! Spite had made him send that vile message. As Javier had pointed out, her future fortune was no secret, and she had always known that Sherman's proposals had stemmed from avarice. He'd seen her as a soft touch, but she wasn't. Just because she'd been free with her generous allowance, happy to pick up the tabs in exchange for fun nights out in smooth, cynically witty company because it had temporarily taken her mind off her unstoppable longing for Javier, didn't mean she was a complete fool.

Thwarted in his plans to get himself a wealthy wife, Sherman was spitefully trying to make mischief.

'Are you all right, my dear?' Lionel Masters was beside her, leaning heavily on his cane, Isabella Maria clinging onto his other arm. 'You are very pale.'

'A bit of a headache.' Zoe pulled herself together. 'Too much champagne, probably.' Her smile felt strained. How could she convince Javier that that note from Sherman was just a cruel attempt to pay her back for consistently turning him down?

The utterly distasteful implications would put her light years away from earning his respect, never mind his love!

'Javier should be taking you on an exotic honeymoon,' Lionel proclaimed. A sentiment echoed by Isabella Maria's 'He should pamper his pretty young bride, I told him as much!' making Zoe feel like something silly and childish marrying a man old enough to be her father. Javier was only twelve years her senior, for goodness' sake, and she wasn't just out of the nursery and her smile was making her face ache!

'We're both perfectly happy here,' she said by way of scotching any more parental interference, neglecting to explain that what use was a honeymoon when the bridegroom had no intention of getting up close and intimate? And even if she'd harboured hopes of making him change his mind in that direction he wouldn't touch her with the proverbial bargepole after what Oliver Sherman had written.

She fell in step beside her in-laws as they progressed slowly towards the house. The caterers were clearing the debris, dismantling the long trestle-table; her wedding day was over. From the corner of her eye she saw Ethel take the gaudy bouquet away— hopefully towards the compost heap!

'Lionel and I will take a rest until supper and give you and Javier some time on your own,' Isabella Maria stated. 'I was surprised and touched when Ethel showed us to the rooms we used when we lived here—I would have thought you and Javier would have chosen them.'

'I chose the blue suite when I came to live here,' Zoe offered obliquely, desperate to get off the subject of sleeping arrangements. 'As far as I know, Javier's never used the master suite. When he came here—' never once since the Spanish disaster '—he used the room above his office for easy access. Now if you'll excuse me, I'll go and find him.'

Easier said than done. A rapid search of the ground-floor rooms, the faithful Boysie at her heels, followed by Honey, the inquisitive ginger cat, revealed nothing but his absence.

Had he taken himself off to fume in private at the discovery that he had got legally tied up to the sort of chick who had been around the block a few times? A flighty piece who would naturally seek forbidden excitement with a former lover when her husband began to bore her?

His proud, fastidious nature would be appalled. That she hadn't exactly given him the impression that she was the type of girl to sit chastely around knitting doilies for her bottom drawer, should Mr Right ever hove into her limited view, made her shudder right down to the soles of her feet.

No, of course not! she scolded herself as she mounted the stairs to seek her room and rid herself of her wedding finery. Get real! Her supposed lack of morals wouldn't touch him emotionally. He'd married her out of his strict sense of duty, hadn't he? Nothing else. He'd decided she was running out of control, and that only by marrying her could he make her toe the line, and that vile note would have reinforced that already entrenched opinion.

Knowing him, and his determination to do the right thing, she'd probably find herself incarcerated in a nunnery for the next two years!

The shadows were softening into hazy dusk as Javier garaged the Jag beside the racy yellow Lotus. Grim satisfaction hardened the sensual line of his mouth. Hooking his discarded suit jacket over his shoulder, he stood to watch the bats' acrobatic aerial display. His thoughts, mercifully calmer now, winged back over the events of the earlier part of the evening.

Sherman would know better than to attempt to contact Zoe again.

A call at his parents' home in the village a couple of miles away had had Monica Sherman, a wispy, fluttery woman, apologizing. 'I'm afraid our son's out. His friends were here earlier and I heard them talking about a new club that's opened just outside Gloucester on the Cheltenham road. I'm sure they decided to try it and that means he won't be in until the early hours—you know what boys are like! Can I give him a message?'

No message, and at around twenty-four Sherman was hardly a boy.

He'd found the club without difficulty. It might be new but the scene had been tediously predictable. Overheated, overcrowded, underlit. Loud, mindless music. He'd located Sherman leaning against a gilded pillar, glass in hand, a cigarette dangling from the corner of his mouth, eyes drooping as he'd ogled a redhead in a yellow dress that had looked little larger than a vest.

Javier had confronted him, his bones clenched, his voice harsh as he'd advised, 'Keep away from my wife. If you know what's good for you, you won't even nod in her direction if you pass her in the street.'

The redhead had giggled. Pique pouting his mouth, Sherman had tried to make himself look taller. Javier had swung away, distaste flattening his mouth. Then had abruptly turned back, going very still as the younger man had sniped, 'You're welcome to her but when your first kid turns up get it DNA-tested to make sure it's yours. Zo's a bit of a goer!'

With one well-aimed blow Javier had felled him. With icy eyes he'd watched the other man slide down the pillar, his arms sheltering his head, his mouth crumpling as if he'd been about to cry and call for his mother!

Javier had turned on his heel and stalked out.

His anger under tight control, he had driven back to Wakeham Lodge, taking extra care to keep within the speed limit. That initial white-hot rage when he had wanted to kill the creep was over. It wasn't like him to resort to violence. In fact it was totally unprecedented. He couldn't understand why he had slapped the little toad when a cutting put-down would have been just as effective and far more dignified.

Logically, the low-life could have been stirring it. And equally logically there was no need to confront Zoe with what her former boyfriend had said. If she had been having sex with him—and it seemed likely in view of the fact that she'd previously announced that she was thinking of accepting his repeated proposals of marriage—his decision to marry her himself to take her out of circulation and keep her safe until she developed at least a modicum of maturity had been the right one.

So why did he suddenly feel empty, as if he was reaching out to find the one thing that would fill the void in his life that was as strange as it was unexpected, not knowing what it was, knowing only that he desperately needed it?

Cynically putting his odd mood down to hunger, he tracked his family down in the conservatory, grouped around the Victorian white-painted cast-iron table lavishly spread with a selection of cold foods.

As he stood unnoticed in the shadows beneath the high arching doorway his breath clogged in his lungs. Zoe had changed into something long, slithery and clingy the colour of old ivory. It left her graceful arms bare and the thigh-high split at the side of the skirt revealed a tantalising glimpse of one elegantly shapely leg.

The light from the amber glass candle-holder near her place-setting flickered across her perfect profile, gilded her pale hair. Something hot and hard balled in his stomach, tightened his loins. The thought of that low-life Sherman mauling her, having sex with her, infiltrated his brain with the red mist of rage.

Sherman had intimated that he hadn't been her only lover. How many had enjoyed that sensual body? Was she hooked on sex?

The memory of her shattering response to the kiss that had started out, on his part, as a simple, caring need to comfort, rapidly becoming something else entirely, leapt with shattering immediacy into his mind. He just about managed to smother a driven groan.

As if his tension had touched her, she turned, her glorious eyes widening, her smile irradiating his veins with the fire of lust. His mouth pulled back against his teeth, he noted the way her breasts peaked against the soft fabric of her dress as she pulled a sharp breath into her lungs and knew he had to have her, claim what was his by right. Receive what had been so freely given to others if Sherman was to be believed.

Fielding his father's, 'Where the hell have you been?' and his mother's accusatory, 'You've been neglecting your bride!' with a smooth, 'I had to attend to a vital piece of business and I'm about to remedy my bride's neglect,' he fastened strong fingers around Zoe's fragile wrist and drew her to her feet.

Her elusive, utterly tantalising perfume made his head spin. The warmth of her sensuous body as she fluidly closed the space between them sent a shaft of driving need through his nervous system, the force of it rocking him back on his heels.

This was about sex. He knew it; she knew it.

It was there in the hazy glow of her golden eyes, the rapid pulse beat at the base of her long creamy throat, the wild rose colour that stole across her cheeks, the erect nipples angled against his chest just below his thundering heart. There in the quiver of heated flesh beneath slinky silk as he scooped her into his arms, tossing over his shoulder as he walked through the doorway, 'I know you'll excuse us. My wife and I have some serious remedying to do.'

CHAPTER THREE

JAVIER hadn't set foot inside the blue suite since Zoe had picked it out for her use when she'd first come to live at Wakeham Lodge. Illuminated as it was by a couple of cream-shaded table lamps, it was like walking into the heart of a cool delphinium, perfect, pristine, no sign of the muddle of strewn discarded clothing or lurid pop-star posters pinned to the walls as he'd automatically expected. Just the softly feminine enclosure of misty blue and the ornate brass bed with its oyster-coloured spread.

He pulled air sharply into his lungs as he conjured up the image of her breathtaking body on that bed. Naked. Willing.

That she was willing was not in dispute here. The moment he'd gathered her up into his arms her own arms had snaked around his neck and stayed there, her head tucked into the angle of his shoulder, just beneath his chin, her body fusing into his as he'd carried her up the stairs.

He could feel the frantic beat of her heart beneath the palm of his left hand, the heat of her smooth thighs beneath his right. As he leant back against the door to close it she lifted her head, her hair brushing like pale, perfumed silk against the hard plane of his cheek. Kissable lips a scant inch away from his. His loins jerked. His eyes closed as he fought the primeval instinct to set her on that bed, drag every scrap of clothing from that delectable body and brand her with his ownership, wipe the memory of all the others from her mind.

Red mist sprang beneath his closed lids. It was a tough call. He opened his eyes as she twisted within his arms, the thrust of her beautiful breasts pressed against his chest in open invitation. An invitation he would have little chance of turning down, he recognised with a savage burst of self-despising. And the first damn thing he saw was the gaudy bouquet from her former lover, glimpsed through the open door that led into the tiny sitting room.

Self-disgust dealt him another swiping blow. His behaviour, the thoughts in his head, put him on a level with Sherman, a man intent on grabbing what he wanted with no thought of the consequences. Zoe might look and act like a woman but she was still a child at heart.

Setting her briskly on her feet, he walked away from her, further into the room, furious with himself for thinking like an animal. She was just a kid. She'd proved it by the casual, almost insultingly off-hand way she'd fallen in with his suggestion that they marry. No adult discussion, no sensible stipulations of her own to make. As if she was viewing the novel idea of wearing a wedding ring as just another experience to be explored. He'd come damn close to giving in to lust and making this marriage a real one—he must have been mad!

A few strides took him past the bed, the centre of his dark, hot thoughts a few moments ago, and on through the wide-open doorway into the sitting room with its chaise upholstered in rich dark blue velvet, the cream marble-topped coffee-table sporting that hateful bouquet. Had she arranged the vulgar blooms herself? Placing them one by one in the crystal vase, remembering the 'fun' she'd had with her lover? Deprived of real love for so many years, had she made sex a substitute?

Was she hooked on it? Could any personable male meet that need? Remembering the thick sizzling shaft of the sex thing when their eyes had clashed down there in the conservatory, he answered his own question.

Watching Javier take the violently coloured roses and lilies, which the misguided Ethel must have arranged, and toss them out of the open window, Zoe felt the weight of rejection settle heavily on her slim shoulders.

She'd been so sure he wanted her, had changed his mind about his wretched paper marriage. The aura around them as he'd carried her up the stairs had been alive with sex, so heady she'd felt intoxicated, convinced that need would follow want on the direct path to love.

She'd hoped that he had the acumen to realise that the message from Ollie had been nothing more than a spite-filled attempt to cause havoc, but he'd only had to see those horrible flowers to make him put her away from him as if she were contaminated material.

The volatile Spanish part of his make-up that had had him hurling the contents of the vase out into the night vanished as he turned back to face her, fastidiously brushing his fingers together, his features wiped of expression as he gave a casual shrug. 'The smell of those lilies was overpowering. They had to go if I'm to get any sleep at all on that sofa. If you had a sentimental attachment to them, then I apologise.'

Zoe's tummy gave a sickening lurch. Her face felt frozen. If he thought his violent disposal of Ollie's flowers had upset her then he was completely off his trolley. It was so unimportant she didn't waste breath on a comment. But, 'Why don't you sleep in your own room? That chaise will be torture.' Act as if you hadn't really expected him to share your bed on your wedding night, she silently adjured herself. Act as if you didn't want it with all your heart, body and soul. She tried to smile and couldn't.

He was unbuttoning his shirt. Zoe's eyes widened as she forced back tears. 'My mother's an early riser,' he imparted prosaically.

Her lovely eyes looked haunted. Had Sherman's bouquet meant that much to her? The hard, hot knot in his gut tightened.

'Mama is incorrigible, as you'll discover when you get to know her better,' he sliced at her. 'Her dearest wish is to hold her grandchildren and if she discovered—and she would, believe me—that we had separate rooms she would raise the dead with her ear-splitting shrieks of outrage. As it is, that little charade downstairs should have put her mind at rest for the moment.'

The shirt was flung over the back of a chair. Zoe's mouth went dry. Faced with six feet plus of masculine power and perfection, bronzed skin covering sleek muscles, she almost exploded with the desperate need to fling her arms around him. Every taut inch of her racked by internal tremors, she resisted the insistent temptation of him.

Been there, done that, she reminded herself hollowly. And he'd run a mile. And the glorious thing that had seemed to spring to pulsating life between them had been a mirage, a charade of his own devising to hide the truth of the kind of marriage they had from his parents.

She had to be very careful to hide her feelings for him, create a part for herself to play, and stick to it. Almost always upfront, her emotions worn on her face and spilling from her tongue, she might find it difficult, but she'd give it her best shot. She had a chance within this sham marriage, maybe only a slim one, granted, but she must not blow it.

Dragging her eyes from him, she turned and made her weakened limbs carry her to the tall set of drawers. The discomfort of trying to fit his big frame on the narrow chaise would be nothing to the way his close proximity would torture her.

Ever since he'd turned from getting rid of Sherman's gaudy flowers she'd been looking stricken, Javier noted grimly. She didn't even have that explicit message to drool over because he'd disposed of that, too. Was she so hooked on sex that she would do what Sherman had suggested and sneak away to be with him to make up for what this marriage lacked? Was she that much of a slut?

'Have you been sleeping with Sherman? Are you aiming to take up his invitation?' His voice came brittly; he had to know. Watching her slim shoulders stiffen, he waited, his eyes narrowing.

The shock of his blunt question kept her rigid, her normally ready tongue stilled to silence. What did he think she was? He'd taken Oliver's vile message on board, that was perfectly obvious. It hurt. It hurt a lot.

Plucking one of the oversized T-shirts she wore to bed from the drawer, she turned then, hurt squeezing her heart until she thought she would choke on it. She wanted to lash out at him, scream and scratch, but she wouldn't allow herself that luxury.

Her voice as sour as vinegar, she pushed out, 'That's my business. I don't ask you if you've slept with all those Glendas and Sophies.' The reminder of how gut-wrenchingly jealous she'd always been of the women who'd briefly shared his life made her feel ill.

Refusing to spare him another glance in case he saw pain in her eyes, she made it to the *en suite* and closed the door behind her.

As he watched her go, the silky fabric of her dress clinging sensually to the shape of her lovely body, Javier's brows met in a dark-as-the-devil frown. Was she criticising his lifestyle when he was supposed to be criticising hers?

But her response had hit home, he recognised guiltily, remembering the times he'd persuaded his current lady to accompany his ward on those holidays he'd promised. Hardly setting a good example, dammit!

Besides, his wild oats were sown. Uncommitted relationships had begun to pall and he'd been celibate for well over a year—but that was an irrelevance, he dismissed as he completed undressing down to his boxer shorts.

What was important was the way she'd avoided answering his question.

Which, in view of all he'd learned, was an answer in itself, he decided with mounting icy fury as he stalked over to one of the windows and stared out at the night, waiting for her to exit the bathroom.

He was going to have to try harder to bring her back in line, make sure she didn't ruin her life. Starting tomorrow.

Sleep had been impossible so he'd spent most of the night working in the office he'd set up here at Wakeham Lodge. Javier rasped a hand over his tough jawline and closed down his computer. It had been light for a couple of hours and the enticing aroma of coffee was beginning to filter through from the kitchen.

He stood up edgily and walked to the window that overlooked the sun-drenched south lawn. His heart jerked. Zoe. Throwing a ball for Boysie. Laughing, long limbs dancing in the early-morning sunlight, long hair flowing down her back like a silky silver-gilt river, flicking across her face. Bare feet, tiny shorts topped by a baggy T-shirt, the soft fabric caught by the breeze that moulded it to those pertly rounded breasts, that tiny waist.

Energetic. A young animal refreshed after hours of untroubled sleep. Just a kid on the brink of woman-hood, blisteringly aware of her own sexuality. He stuffed his fists into his trouser pockets. In dire need of taming. A driven groan escaped him. What kind of guy tied himself to that kind of responsibility?

The answer came as she scooped the wriggling little dog up into her arms and buried her face in its hairy ruff.

A guy who cared. Who had always cared.

A muscle jerked at the side of his hard jaw. He turned and strode from the room, heading for a shower, a shave and a change of clothes.

There was nothing remotely childlike about the Zoe who presented herself for breakfast an hour later. The sleeveless shift dress in a heavy cream-coloured cotton was both casual and classy, perfect for a country house breakfast with the in-laws. Her glorious hair was smoothly coiled into her nape, emphasising the purity of her profile, and the narrow hem of her dress just covered her knees, but rode just above as she took her seat at the table.

Javier felt his throat close up. Serene, elegant, poised. But hellishly sexy. It screamed at him. He didn't want to hear it.

He didn't want to watch the curve of her lush mouth as she drank from her glass of orange juice, but he did. Those smiling golden eyes behind the ridiculously thick fringing lashes moved confidently between his parents as the light conversation passed over the eggs and racks of hot toast. He waited for those eyes to turn his way but they didn't. He found himself willing her to look at him, but she didn't, and cursed himself for a fool, losing control of the situation to the calm, surprisingly adult sexy witch sitting opposite.

She even managed a perfect, enigmatic smile when his mother archly enquired if she had slept well. He'd expected a raging blush or a sulky pout at the uncomfortable memory of what had passed between them.

His wife was starting to surprise him he recognised with a not unpleasant lurch of his gut.

'I regret that Lionel and I have to leave today.' Isabella Maria assumed a sorrowful expression, but her black eyes were dancing as she turned towards her son. 'But I'm sure regret will be very far from your mind as you wave us on our way!' She laid down her linen napkin, preparing to leave the table. 'You must promise to bring Zoe to our summer home for a long visit. She will enjoy the views, the mountain air, you know she will. I am sure the business will survive if you are not poking your nose into every aspect every minute of every day, *sí*?'

Leaning back in his chair, Javier hooked his hands behind his head. Smiled, gave every appearance of being totally relaxed when rivers of a peculiar kind of tension were scalding in his veins. Drawled, 'I make my own plans, Mama. As you know.'

His plans for Zoe had nothing to do with lazy, sybaritic days and long, perfumed nights. He didn't go looking for trouble! A lazy brow arched. 'Do you need help with your packing?'

A little under two hours later they projected a united front, the archetypal just-married couple as they waved goodbye to Javier's parents. As the car Lionel had hired for the visit disappeared round the final bend Zoe just knew what would happen.

Javier stepped abruptly away, his arm dropping

from around her shoulders. Emptiness washed through her like a chilling wave.

Even though she knew the display of closeness had been for his parents' benefit she had treasured every moment, every smile, every touch and soft word. She felt sick with loss but he mustn't know that. Javier believed she was still a rebellious brat, running out of control. The only way to disabuse him, show him that she was a grown woman, worthy of his respect for starters, adult female to adult male, was to do her utmost to tailor her behaviour to what he least expected from the bolshie teenager he saw her as.

Giving him the merest glance, her slight smile serene, she murmured, 'I'm sorry to see your parents go, they're darlings. But at least we can dispense with the play-acting. You must have found it a strain.'

Strangely enough, he hadn't. Javier's eyes narrowed on her delectable profile.

'It's such a beautiful day.' A small, self-contained smile was aimed somewhere behind his left shoulder. 'I think I'll take a walk.'

In Sherman's direction? Javier's eyes snapped. No way! A strong hand descended on her shoulder before she could make good her intentions.

'You need to pack,' he stated firmly. 'I want to leave for the London apartment before noon.'

This time Zoe looked directly at him, a frown peaking her brows above dismayed eyes. The city would be alien, hot and airless, clogged with traffic and tourists, and, 'Boysie,' she objected. 'I can't leave him, he'll really miss me. He'd been abandoned when I found him—he'll think it's happening all over again!'

Quite apart from the likelihood of the little dog pining, here, with vast expanses of countryside to lose herself in, the home she was now totally comfortable with, she could hold her own in this strange marriage. She could take a crash course of driving lessons with a professional to pass some of the time, decide on a career as backup if her hopes to be a real wife to Javier, mother of his children, came to nothing. 'Why can't we stay here?' she asked, her voice rising with desperation.

Any excuse to stick around, close to her lover? Every nerve in Javier's body tightened. 'The dog will be·fine,' he incised, holding onto his temper, hating the shaft of jealousy that churned his insides. He had never been jealous of anyone in his entire life. He sure as hell wasn't starting now! 'Will Ethel neglect to feed him? Will Joe kick him?'

His obvious sarcasm stinging, Zoe had to admit that he was right on that point. Both Ethel and Joe doted on the dog. Not wanting to leave him had just been an excuse. A poor one, too, she conceded as he told her firmly, 'The world doesn't owe me a living, I have to work.'

A dig at her? Did he think she was a parasite, content to live off the wealth her father had worked his socks off to accumulate? Her spine stiffened even as she felt hot colour flood her cheeks. She would just have to show him differently!

'I could work from here,' he conceded bluntly. 'But don't forget, the Ramsays were originally employed by my parents. There's a strong bond of loyalty. As you'll have noticed they've always been treated like part of the family. My dear mama will be on the phone on a daily basis, checking up on the newly-weds! We can't hide separate rooms from Ethel and I'll be damned if I'm going to bed down on that uncomfortable sofa for the foreseeable future.'

Her lovely mouth was sulky, her eyes downcast. In the sunlight her hair was the colour of champagne. His throat constricted and his voice emerged thickly, gently. 'Start packing. And if it eases your conscience, we can visit your pets each weekend. I can put up with that sofa for one night out of seven.' And make sure she didn't wander Sherman-wards.

It was the voice of a man humouring a child, making concessions in return for good behaviour, Zoe recognised, furious with herself. Her error had been in making that instinctive objection in the first place. Her head coming up, a slight smile in place, she remedied it. 'I hadn't looked at it in that light. You're right, of course. Ethel's got sharp eyes and it would be difficult to keep up a lovey-dovey act for her benefit. Drive us both insane.' The smile slanted wider as unconcealed surprise glinted in his eyes. 'I'll go and pack.'

The London apartment was just as she remembered it from the overnight stay before she and Javier had flown out to Spain that Easter. She'd taken in every detail with eyes greedy for everything that made up his personal space.

The plastic-card-activated lift took them directly to the foyer, cool off-white walls, a single Venetian salon chair, a mahogany door that led into a long sitting room, one wall entirely of glass giving fabulous views over the city. A minimum amount of furniture, understated, expensive, classy. It needed a woman's touch, Zoe thought now as she'd thought then, when her feet had first touched the bland oatmeal-coloured carpet. Flowers, jewel-coloured cushions, bright paintings to break the severity, a clutter of magazines and books to make it look more home-like.

Was this to be her home for the next two years? Sterile, to suit a sterile marriage? Her stomach curdled. Then she railed at herself for being such a wimp. Two years gave her enough time to make him fall in love with her!

Taking her small suitcase from him, she told him calmly, 'I take it I'll be using the room I had before? I remember the way.' She gave him the smallest glance. Too dangerous to allow her eyes to linger on her stunningly gorgeous new husband. He made her heart turn over, pound and clatter, drying up her throat, made the softness of love shine from her far-too-revealing eyes. She'd once made the crass mistake of telling him she loved him. By now he would have written it off as silly girlish infatuation. Let him keep his misconception.

Almost as soon as she had started to walk away she turned again to face him, very slowly. 'Look, I'm fully aware of why you married me, Javier—to stop me making a fool of myself with unsuitable people. I admire your sense of duty.'

Was there a trace of utter wickedness as her sexy mouth curved in a slight smile that held his fascinated gaze? Probably. She could be a witch when she wanted to be.

'And I accepted because it was a way out of an empty, pointless life.' Amazed that her face hadn't gone fierily red at the outright lie, Zoe reminded with commendable cool, 'You offered your guidance. And I'll take it. But we need to discuss my place in this marriage. This evening, if you have no other plans?'

Definitely a challenge in those beautiful golden eyes. A sexual challenge? Something gave a violent wrench inside him. Was she about to tell him that she wanted her place to be in his bed? Watching the sensual sway of her body as she finally walked to the door that accessed the rest of the penthouse apartment, he wondered if he would have the strength to resist.

His breath felt hot in his lungs. The way the little minx could get under his skin was beginning to seriously annoy him. Behaving with natural, almost childlike innocence at one moment, sulking because he was keeping her away from her lover the next, then acting like a poised adult.

And all the time the undercurrent of hot sex...

His smoky eyes grim, he stalked after her. No one was going to run rings round him! They could have that discussion right here and now. And if she so much as hinted at a desire to make this marriage a real one he'd shoot her down in flames and throw the fire extinguisher straight out of the window.

He didn't knock. Just walked right in. Her suitcase was open on the bed. And in answer to his terse question, she merely straightened, hooked a strand of silky hair behind one ear and gave him the bland smile that made him grind his teeth because it just made him want to use his own mouth to ravage it away, and casually answered him, 'I'm your wife. I only wanted to know whether you expect me to do wifely things—cook your meals, iron your shirts, that sort of stuff.'

Minutes later, closing the door of his home office behind him, Javier couldn't remember what answer he'd given back. None, probably.

And just why had her prosaic reply—the last thing he'd expected to hear—flooded him with cold disappointment?

CHAPTER FOUR

ENTERING the silent apartment, Zoe dropped her handbag on the nearest coffee-table and walked out of her high heels. Once again the long evening stretched emptily ahead and depression settled heavily on her slim shoulders.

Next month they would be celebrating their first wedding anniversary, though celebrating was hardly the word to use, she amended with a tight laugh that wasn't a laugh at all. Halfway through the time Javier had allotted their marriage. And what, exactly, had she achieved?

Zilch! In fact, the miracle of having Javier fall headlong in love with her simply wasn't going to happen and she might as well face it.

Her shoulders drooping, she walked through to her bedroom on leaden legs. She'd given it her best shot, turned herself inside out trying to become special to him, a woman he could respect, admire—a woman he could find desirable and eventually grow to love.

Getting out of her tailored primrose-yellow suit, she took her usual quick shower and dressed in light cotton trousers and toning dark green shirt, avoiding her eyes in the mirror because she couldn't bear to see defeat looking back at her.

She knew she should make herself something to eat but couldn't be bothered. She'd have something to drink when she'd glanced at the post that had arrived after she'd left. A couple of bills, a letter for Javier addressed in a flowing female hand and something for her.

An invitation to Guy and Jenny's wedding. She must have been an afterthought because the ceremony was to take place this coming weekend, she decided with a wry smile. Javier had effectively taken her out of circulation, so her friends would have as good as forgotten about her.

The ceremony was to be held at the village church, she noted, the reception at the White Boar.

So those two had decided to formalise their sizzling relationship—they would have a proper marriage…

Unlike hers.

And she'd have to pass. Javier had made no secret of his dislike and distrust of her wild friends. She laid the invitation back on the pile of post awaiting Javier's return and the wall-mounted phone rang as she was reaching for a carton of fruit juice from the fridge.

Javier!

Her stupid heart gave its all-too-familiar lurch. He always phoned from his hotel room at around this time when he was working away, a state of affairs that had become far more frequent over the past three months.

Checking up on her? What else? Certainly not for the pleasure of hearing her voice!

'How was your day?'

'Fine.' Her reply was just as predictable, as was the potted run-down that he always expected her to give.

Reminiscent of a father asking a child what it had done at school all day.

'The usual Thursday afternoon meeting,' she told him dully. He'd been instrumental in getting her on the committee of a charity working with the home-less, and she'd found the work challenging, absorbing and deeply rewarding, but the enthusiasm was miss-ing from her voice today as she enlightened him. 'We're in the throes of organising a late autumn fund-raising thrash; you'll have to dragoon your wealthy friends into buying tickets. They'll cost an arm and a leg.'

Acid in her voice there? Probably.

During the first months of their paper marriage she'd been introduced to his circle of high-flying friends. Sophisticated dinner parties mostly, the spiky chatter way over her head, an odd overheard remark about child brides and the common sense of marrying for money even if one did already have simply oodles of one's own, dahling.

She'd been put under the microscope and had en-dured it with outward serenity to please Javier. She hadn't gone off on one—

'I thought I'd be able to make it back in time to go to Wakeham as usual on Saturday morning.' She tuned in to what he was saying.

She could hear voices in the background, the husky sound of female laughter. He was entertaining. People he'd met while checking up on progress at the site? Or was the husky woman his regular travelling companion? she wondered on a sickening surge of jealousy.

'But something's come up, so I'm afraid I'll be stuck here in Cannes until some time next week. So,' he came out with the next stock question, 'what are you doing this evening?'

As if he cared! She swallowed hard on the rising bubble of rage. Stuck in Cannes—oh, what a terrible shame! Throwing a party in his hotel suite—oh, how absolutely dreadful for him! No doubt being hit on by some fascinating full-blown woman—oh, she could weep for him, poor darling!

Zoe bit back the sarcastic comments and instead of telling the boring truth—ironing, reading or watching something on TV; what else was she to do?—she fibbed tightly, 'I'm going out. Hitting the town and seeing what turns up. See you next week, then.' And cut the connection and burst into tears.

By the time she'd used the last tissue in the box Zoe was struggling to pull herself together. She had to get right down to face a few unpleasant facts. Such as it was time she started living in the real world and stopped inhabiting a dream that had no chance of coming true.

For the last eleven months she'd been sweetness and light, never complaining, not even when he'd grown more and more remote, his eyes turning to brooding charcoal whenever he happened to look at her, regularly jetting off to sites all over the world. Leaving her to—

Miss him so badly she ached all over.

Instead of getting despondent over the way things were turning out, she'd gritted her teeth and clung onto her new maturity, thrown herself into her charity work, planned the welcome-home dinner she'd cook, stored up amusing anecdotes to entertain him with, shopped for the restrained and classy clothes she knew he preferred his women to wear...

His women!

He was a highly sexed male animal. Sophie—or had it been Glenda?—had actually and hatefully boasted of that fact during a session of babysitting holiday duties. She hadn't wanted to hear that, she remembered, had been physically sick with jealousy.

Had he found a new woman to satisfy his needs? That would explain his increasing absences, wouldn't it? The woman whose husky laughter she'd heard in the background only minutes ago! While his wife sat meekly at home, untouched, pure and properly behaved!

Well, not any more! It was time she cut free, saved herself a load of heartache. Acknowledged finally that what she had hoped for would never happen. Javier would never see her as a real woman, a woman he could fall in love with. To him she would always remain in permanent childhood, a self-inflicted duty. Something he would put up with until she came into her inheritance and could be trusted to behave sensibly!

Her golden eyes sparking rebelliously, her stomach churning sickly with a horrible mixture of jealousy and hopelessness, she punched in the Wakeham Lodge number and when it was picked up launched straight in.

'Ethel, I'll be driving down tomorrow. No, Javier won't be with me, he's working in France. I'm going to a local wedding on Saturday —you remember Guy and Jenny? And I'll probably stay at Wakeham until the middle of next week.'

And Javier, returning to an empty apartment, could make what he liked of that. As for her, she was going out. This sham of a marriage was over.

Nearly midnight, and the wedding party was still going full blast. Lights strobed, moody blues and purples, couples dancing to the frenetic music. There were mostly young people left, the older guests having called it a night a couple of hours ago, the newlyweds having left for their honeymoon well before that.

Jenny had looked fantastic in her beautiful wedding gown. The adoration between the couple as they'd exchanged their marriage vows had been real enough to reach out and touch.

So different from her own wedding, almost a year ago. Zoe's eyes misted as her throat tightened. She swallowed hard. She wouldn't look back to the futile, juvenile hopes she'd harboured at that time. She would not! It was time to move on. Tonight was the start of the process.

And she'd been having fun, hadn't she? Of course she had!

In the early evening, after the wedding breakfast, she'd changed here at the White Boar hotel from the summery suit she'd worn to the church service into a flirty scarlet chiffon dress with a dipping halter neckline, a narrow waist and a short flared skirt that made dancing a pleasure, freeing her movements. And it had been great to catch up with friends she hadn't seen for a year.

Pleading aching feet, she'd rid herself of the latest batch of would-be partners, excused herself when they'd shown the inclination to linger. She'd had fun but it was time to get back to Wakeham and spend the next few days considering her future, walking the dog and generally chilling out.

Placing her glass of iced water on one of the small tables that bordered the banquet hall, she felt hard fingers bite into her wrist.

'Been avoiding me, Zo? Given hubby the slip?'

Oliver. As the answer to both questions was obvious and affirmative she didn't bother to answer. Just, 'Let go of me, please.'

He didn't. Simply tugged her closer. He was sweating. He looked drunk. It had been over twelve months since she'd last seen him. In that time his pretty-boy features had grown blurred, his waistline hinting at an incipient paunch. Shock stilled her tongue; in any case it was pointless to tear him off a strip for that vile message he'd sent with those horrible flowers. It all seemed part of a different life…

'Nothing to say to an old mucker?' Whisky fumes soured his breath. 'Ever wondered what you'd missed when you turned me down?'

'Never!' The more she tried to pull free, the harder his fingers gripped. And no one was taking any notice. Dim lighting and everyone absorbed in dancing to something slow and smoochy now, locked together, clinging, totally oblivious.

'Then what say I show you?' His free hand dived

beneath her halter top, hot and sweaty, squeezing, hurting. Her raised knee didn't have time to connect in self-defence before he had her off balance, thrust back against the wall, a heavy thigh pushed between her shaking legs, his hands all over her, making her want to retch.

And then, like a miracle, she was free, Oliver hurtling backwards, falling against one of the tables. She was panting, her breath coming in shallow frightened gasps. Her eyes felt so dazed she could scarcely see. She forced them wide. Was she facing a knight in shining armour or an even greater threat?

Javier!

Big, dark and coldly furious.

Relief washed through her in huge convulsive waves. Levering herself away from the wall, she laved her dry lips with the tip of her tongue and shakily blurted the first thing that came into her head. 'I thought you said you wouldn't be back for days.'

'Obviously.' His voice was dryer than a Saharan wind. The background music picked up in tempo. Oliver, she noted, had scuttled away. Javier said, 'Out!' and jerked his head in the direction of the doorway.

Glad to, Zoe headed for the exit to the hotel foyer, her scarlet skirts swaying around her long legs, aware of his eyes pinned on her. She had never been so happy to see anyone in her life, and as soon as they reached the well-lit foyer, the relative silence, she turned to him, the colour she'd lost starting to steal back into her face. 'Thanks. I'll just fetch my things.'

She sounded breathless, she knew she did; she had

hardly been able to get those few words out. Her whole body was shaking with reaction. She turned jerkily towards the lift that would take her to the room she had changed in after the wedding breakfast, unprepared for his, 'Not now. I want you out of here.'

His words felt like bullets in his throat. Anger and hostility burned in his brain. He had never lifted a finger against a woman in his life, never wanted to. But now he wanted to turn her over his knee and paddle her delightful backside! But he would never betray his honour by doing any such thing.

An insistent hand on the small of her back was sufficient to guide her unresistant body out through the main doors, into the quiet night. There was nothing quiet about his thoughts. How long had Sherman and his wife been mauling each other, propped up against that wall? How long before the two of them would have sneaked away to somewhere more private?

'Get in.' He opened the passenger door of his Jaguar. Zoe lifted her head to look into his face. All hard angles and sharp planes, his eyes like lasers. She had never faced such savage anger before. Her throat went dry. No knight to the rescue. More like an avenging angel.

She shivered as the night air cooled her overheated skin, pulling herself together, remembering that he was no longer part of her life. 'I've got my own car.' The Lotus, parked right beside his, he couldn't have failed to see it. 'The keys are in my hotel room. I'm going back to get them and check out. You can't tell me what to do, not any more. The stupid farce of our marriage is over.'

Javier ignored that. He picked up on the damning evidence, and his voice pulsed with outrage. 'Then it's a pity you and Sherman didn't use the room you'd booked instead of having sex in full view of half the county.' He dragged in a tight breath. 'Get in.'

In this mood there was no talking to him, Zoe recognised, her heart sinking. Just for a moment she'd had the fleeting thought that, not believing he was rescuing her from a hateful, scary situation, he'd actually been jealous. Not the case. Hadn't she learned enough during the last eleven months to stop herself hoping for the impossible? The primary source of his anger stemmed from what people might say about his wife's behaviour, making him look like a cuckolded fool! How he would loathe that!

Wordlessly, she folded herself into the seat, shuddered as he slammed the door closed and hated him for the power he had to hurt her time after time. Then as he took his seat behind the steering wheel she asked in a viciously tight voice, 'So what brought you back from the delights of Cannes?'

'Your stated intent to go out on the prowl,' he shot back tersely as he fired the powerful engine.

Recalling the rebellious lie didn't make her feel guilty. Quite the opposite. Folding her arms across her chest as he pulled out of the hotel car park, she fumed, 'It's all right for you to do as you please, go where you like, hang out with other people—women, as far as I know. But I must sit in an empty apartment twiddling my thumbs, is that it?'

Accelerating, he growled, 'Grow up, Zoe!'

'I am,' Zoe shot at him through gritted teeth. 'I'm taking charge of my own life from now on. I'm not a child, in case you hadn't noticed! And I won't be treated like one.'

It wasn't the way she'd wanted to end it. Not in an undignified spat with him losing all patience with her. She'd intended to tell him of her decision to end the sham of their marriage before schedule coolly and civilly, explain that he had no need to worry about her, thanks to him she was on track. But what he'd walked in on had put paid to that.

Subsiding into miserable silence as the explosive tension coming from him in almost tangible waves made her bones shake, made her remember the times his patience had seemed inexhaustible.

Learning to drive in London when they'd first been married. Apart from sessions with qualified instructors Javier had taken her out time after time to practise the dreaded parallel parking. Calm, good-humoured and above all patient when she'd repeatedly, session after session, got it all wrong. Spending what must have been hours with her until she'd eventually got the hang of the manoeuvre.

To celebrate passing her driving test at the first attempt he'd bought her what she'd privately called a granny-going-shopping car, sedate and sensible. Not like the Lotus.

Thinking of those happier times, innocent and improbably naive times, when she'd hoped that their marriage would turn into a real one, made her want to cry.

So she injected steel into her spine when the short journey was completed and she exited the car and found to her shame that her legs would barely hold her upright.

As the security lights came on Zoe leant against the side of the car for much-needed support and watched Javier unlock the front door. She was shaking again, but with rage this time. How dared he think she'd arranged to spend the night with Oliver Sherman?

To immediately leap to that conclusion—not even bothering to ask for her side of the sordid story—had to mean that his opinion of her morals was solid rock-bottom!

Had he always thought she was a slag?

Her head high, she walked into the house, passing him without so much as a glance, and on up the stairs, her soft mouth tightly compressed to hold back the scalding words of self-defence that were blistering her tongue. Throw them at him and it would all come out—the stark truth that she had never slept with Oliver Sherman, or any other man. The pathetic fact that he, Javier, was the only man she'd ever wanted.

A savage thrust of anger made Javier's heart thump against his chest as his narrowed eyes followed her progress. The scarlet dress was a come-on if ever he'd seen one, making the most of her glorious man-teaser body, emphasising the sexy curve of her hips and the length of her shapely legs.

Had the minx bought it especially for her assignation with Sherman? And how many times, during his absences, had the two of them been together? His teeth grated, tightening his rock-hard jaw. He shouldn't have left her to her own devices, her own inclinations. Once again he'd solved the problem he'd faced by withdrawing. This time not to allow his absence to cool her ardour, but his own!

He took the stairs two at a time. To hell with cool, gentlemanly withdrawal—that solution had been born of his pragmatic English genes. The Spaniard in him demanded confrontation, the airing of the emotions that were turning his insides to fire.

Her bedroom was empty, just the teasing subtle ghost of the perfume she wore and the muted sound of the shower. His hands stuffed in the pockets of his tailored trousers, he paced the floor, feeling the tiger inside his chest try to claw its way out.

Her statement that she was about to go out on the town had rung alarm bells loud and clear. He'd packed four days' worth of meetings into two and flown back to London. And waited. Her car hadn't been in the underground parking area and the wedding invitation had told him where she'd be.

He should have known the new butter-wouldn't-melt persona was just an act!

The cool blue pristine bedroom, the ornate bed with its smooth cream cover, mocked him. She was a normal healthy young adult. She had a sex drive like anyone else. A frustrated sex drive. Despite her volunteer charity work, to which he had to admit she'd willingly and enthusiastically given large chunks of her time, she'd been bored within the sterile bounds of their marriage and had taken up the invitation her former lover had issued.

With hot enthusiasm?

A groan vented through his clenched teeth. She was his wife, dammit!

As if on cue the object of his fevered thoughts exited the bathroom. Water darkened her hair, slicked her silky skin; the towel around her body was tiny. Golden eyes widened with shock, lush lips parting. Her breathing accelerated, exposing the tops of her full breasts as they thrust against the towelling barrier.

The thought of Sherman luxuriating in that sensational body filled him with blistering anger. Sherman had entered that heaven on earth while he had behaved like the perfect gentleman, putting on that cool façade while every move the little witch made him want her more, absenting himself, putting temptation behind him. What kind of man did that make him?

'You dishonour me!' His Spanish genes came to the fore as he spoke with savage contempt. 'My wife making a cuckold of me in front of an audience! Are you always so indiscreet? Or were you both too drunk to care? His breath would have made a distillery smell like fresh sea air!'

Eyes darkening to pitch castigated her. Zoe threw sparks of loathing back at him. How dared he?

And perhaps the most crushing thing to come out of this was the painfully obvious fact that his gripe had little to do with his premise that she and Oliver had been having sex, but a lot to do with their lack of discretion!

Reining back the wild-cat impulse to slap those strong dark features cost more in self-control than he would ever know. Hitching the towel more securely around her tense body, she came back with a cool that took a huge mental effort to achieve. 'If that's what you think of me then you'll be happy to know that I won't dishonour your name any longer than it takes to get an annulment. And I have never been your true wife!'

Smouldering charcoal clashed with molten gold. In his anger he was dangerously exciting. Despite all her best intentions her body thrummed with it, betraying her. Her throat felt thick. She tried to swallow and couldn't.

Electrifying tension pulsed in the air, thickening it, making it difficult to breathe. Zoe's fingers tightened on the slipping towel. Her long-standing relationship with this hard-angled man now seemed completely unstable. Every muscle of his powerful lean body was rigid with the internal battle she sensed within him.

Her soft mouth trembled as ice shivered down her spine while, simultaneously, violently contrasting heat coursed through her veins. His veiled eyes fastened on the betrayal of her lips. It was like a caress, soft and invasive.

She snatched air into her lungs and he took a slow pace forward, his own mouth softening from the harsh line of contempt. She watched it happen and her lower limbs became unsteady. His brooding eyes, locked still on her suddenly unbearably sensitised mouth, gave him away.

Her breath caught again as the prickly sensation between her thighs turned hot and liquid. Something throbbed, fiery, pagan and insistent. Zoe knew she should ask him to leave, tell him they could talk about the ending of their marriage in the morning when they were both calmer, but she couldn't form the words.

'As you said, you have never been my true wife. I've kept my hands off you, even though I've been tempted to do exactly the opposite,' he informed her with a raw edge to his voice. 'I told myself you were too young to know what you wanted but, as you pointed out, you are no longer a child.'

Zoe swallowed convulsively. She'd thought he was totally indifferent but he had wanted her. He'd said so. Her heart drummed a tattoo in her throat. He had advanced until he was a hand's breadth away. Thick ebony lashes veiled eyes that were still fixated on her mouth.

'If you wanted sex you should have told me,' he informed her with force. 'I would have been happy to oblige; there would have been no reason for you to offer the freedom of your body to another man.'

Zoe's long lashes flickered. He was volatile, unpredictable, displaying a side of his character she had never been allowed to see. Breath hissed from her straining lungs and the tip of her tongue moved languorously over her lips, moistening the dryness.

'I didn't—' she started to protest, but her voice died when she saw fierce determination settle on his charismatic features and heard the banked-down husk of emotion in his voice as a hand flicked out to move strands of damp hair from their resting place between her breasts. 'You want sex? Tell me.'

A forefinger tracked the place where her hair had lain. Zoe shuddered convulsively.

'Well?' he pressed. There was a flare of hot desire

in his eyes and the clean male scent of him was a further aphrodisiac. She didn't need it! She already felt as if she had overdosed on the potent stuff! 'Answer me.' The command was issued thickly.

'Not like this,' she managed. She sounded like someone being tortured, she recognised. 'Not—not when you hate me.'

His long mouth curved in what passed for a smile. 'I don't hate you. I hate the sin but not the sinner—hang onto that thought while I try to get an answer to my question.'

For a moment she didn't understand. Enlightenment came when he raised both hands to cup her naked shoulders, his thumbs gently rotating against the tender hollows beneath. 'Tell me to stop touching you, and I will.'

Zoe gasped for breath. How long had she ached for his touch? Years and years. He was convinced she was little better than a common whore. She should have enough pride to walk away from him. She couldn't move; she had no pride where he was concerned.

'No?' His breath feathered the top of her downbent head. 'Not yet?' He felt her flesh quiver beneath his hands. He wasn't proud of what he was doing. He felt uncontrollably driven. Driven by desire. Months ago he'd recognised the edginess he felt in her presence for what it really was and had taken steps to remove himself from the temptation of her. Reminding himself that sex wasn't part of the bargain they'd made…that she was too immature…that he'd be taking unfair advantage…

Now things were different. His earlier suspicions of her promiscuity were confirmed. It should have made him turn his back on her for all time. But it hadn't.

He wanted to put his brand of ownership on her, turn her off every man she'd ever had sex with for the rest of her life. She was his wife, dammit!

He smothered a groan. His hands slid lower, fingers sliding over the upper curves of her partially naked breasts. Blood was thundering hotly in his ears. But if she told him to back off he would.

Immediately.

Walk out and leave her to go for that annulment.

Her skin felt like the softest satin. The firm globes hardening in response to his touch, sending him insane. 'Not yet?' The repeated question was thick with his need.

Zoe made a soft whimpering sound at the back of her throat. The lingering touch of his lean fingers, his closeness, were playing havoc with her ability to think. His eyes had turned to smoke, hot with desire. He wanted her. He ignited her.

Aided by his fingers, the towel dropped to the floor. Another step closer, another turn of the screw. She felt a long shudder rake through his body, so close to hers she could feel the potent male strength and heat of him, sense the heavy pounding of his heart. How often had she fantasised about him touching her naked body? Countless. But she had never known it could be this wonderful.

His lean hands not quite steady, Javier lifted both of them and tilted her face towards him. Her eyes

were glazed gold, siren-hot, half hidden by the heavy
sweep of her dark lashes. She shifted her feet a little,
like a sleepwalker. The burning, hard tips of her beautiful breasts were touching his shirt, searing him
through the fine material. His body was one long ache
for her and he didn't know how much longer he could
hang onto his control. The decision had to be hers.

'Do I stop this?' he asked, hardly able to breathe.
'Tell me.'

CHAPTER FIVE

ZOE'S body throbbed with desire and his did, too—she could feel it. A major miracle had happened! Javier actually saw her as a woman, not as a needy child or a pesky adolescent, and he wanted her!

Add love to her side of the equation and there was no backing off, no denying herself what she had craved for long, empty years.

Did it matter what he thought of her? Wasn't half a loaf better than no bread? Wasn't this—him, her love for him—the only thing of any importance?

Lifting her hands, Zoe pulled his head down to hers, her mouth giving him his answer. I love him like crazy, was her last sane thought when, after a nanosecond of stony stillness, he groaned deep in his throat and kissed her back.

Kissed her with fierce passion, ravaging her mouth with his brand of possession, kissed her until she was drugged and breathless, craving the next intimate slide of his tongue, returning it with interest, clinging, her arms around his neck, hands sliding through the crisp blackness of his hair, her body on fire, almost exploding as his hands took off on a hungry quest to explore her willing and wanton nakedness.

His body shook as she lifted herself onto her toes, the eager arc of her hips lifted to meet the burning, insistent pressure of his. She melted into him as though she belonged. His heartbeat thundered as the irresistible force of desire intensified to primal need.

The provocative minx was turning the tables, branding him with her mark. She had made him jettison his self-respect as if it had no more worth than an old paper bag! He had no more self-control where she was concerned now than a newborn baby.

Her pouting lips were teasing now, feathering tiny tasting kisses at the corner of his mouth, grazing down to the underside of his jaw, her elegantly lovely hands slowly parting his shirt buttons.

Everything seemed to be happening in slow motion, every atom of his being centred on what was happening here, the feel of her silky skin beneath his hands, the exquisite curve where her hips flared from her tiny waist, the scent of her, the pulsating, addictive warmth of her flesh. In a moment those perfectly formed, sinfully tight breasts would be touching his naked skin.

He was sweating, shaking with need. Lust. Knowing what she was should have had him fastidiously turning his back on her.

She was a witch. Had to be.

He was bewitched. Glad to be.

Those exquisitely delicate hands at last tugged his shirt free of the waistband of his trousers, the backs of her fingers sliding against his overheated skin. Javier couldn't breathe.

She was offering what he'd craved for long, tormenting months. Months of doing the honourable thing, of removing himself from temptation as much as possible.

The events of this evening had ejected honour right out of the window.

He heard the tiny mew of her satisfaction as pebble-hard nipples rubbed against the tight drum that was his near-exploding chest and expelled a driven sigh that seemed to come up from the soles of his feet, before lifting her in his arms and carrying her with long, impatient strides to the waiting bed with its mocking smooth virginal covers.

She was his wife, dammit to hell and back again!

Her arms clung; she was boneless, fluid. Her beautiful golden eyes were glazed with passion, enticing, inviting, sending him out of his mind. She was avid for what he could give her and he needed it more than he'd ever needed anything!

She was heaven, spread out on that bed. Her long pale hair spilling over the pillow, her lush lips parted as her breath came in rapid, shallow pants. On driven impulse, Javier bent over her and took one rosy distended nipple into his mouth just briefly and then the other, his pulses surging as her back arched in wanton response, her hands reaching for him.

He stood back, avoiding the supplication of her outstretched arms. It took one hell of a lot of will power. He wanted to possess his wife—his woman— right now. But two could tease. She didn't have the monopoly on driving the opposite sex crazy. He shed the rest of his clothes very slowly. Her witchy yellow eyes drank in every movement.

Siren's eyes.

Pulling him to her. The air was hot, full of sex, the

awareness between the two of them more intense than anything he'd ever experienced.

Naked, he joined her. She writhed towards him, threading her fingers through his hair, pulling him to her like the experienced wanton she was, slick skin fusing with the heat of his.

Javier took both her hands in his and held them above her head. Long mouth twisted in a wry smile, his eyes hot smoke, he began to stroke lazily tormenting kisses over her breasts, down to the soft curve of her tummy. She squirmed in wild ecstasy, frantic need, her fingers digging into his shoulders, her hips lifting for him, her breathing out of control.

Javier gave her a grim smile and, before moving his dark head lower, told her, 'Patience. I'm in no hurry. I've waited a long time, and I fully intend to savour every slow second…'

The soft light of dawn was filtering through the open window. Birdsong woke her with liquid silvery notes. Her lips curved with blissful contentment, her eyes turning to him, to his smooth, muscular back packaged in taut golden skin. A hand reached out to touch. She withdrew it, her smile widening. After last night he would need all the rest he could get.

Last night. If her body didn't ache in all sorts of unaccustomed places she would have believed it to have been a dream, a precious fantasy.

Her heart swelled within her breast. No dream. It had been real and way beyond and above mere perfection. A delicious tremor rippled through her as she recalled that one short moment when he might have denied her.

When he had finally, for the first time, parted her thighs and entered the place he had made so ready, thrusting his swollen length so deeply within her she hadn't been able to disguise the sharp gasp of pain as the barrier had been broken.

Javier had gone still. Very still. Had lifted his head. 'Zoe, you're—'

'Yes.'

'I—'

'Don't talk!' A command bordering on panic. Not prepared to let him get all protectively honourable, not now, she wrapped her legs tightly around his body and that decisive movement let him know she was giving him everything, all she was, all she had ever been.

And he gave, too. Gave heaven on earth.

He stirred. Zoe's body stirred in response. She touched him then, the pads of the fingers of one hand tracing a loving path down his back.

He went still, seemed to stop breathing, then turned, met those melting, slumberous golden eyes and his heart contracted. 'Zoe—' He reached out to touch his fingers to the side of her adorable face, his dark brows clenching as she gave him her glorious smile, arched closer and wrapped her long legs around his.

His for the taking.

Guilt swamped him.

He reached for the hands that were already creating havoc as they palmed the blatant evidence of what she did to him, held them in his fists between their bodies.

Javier knew he should move, shatter this incredible feeling of intimacy. What he had to say to her would banish the bloom from her lovely face, turn the soft light in her eyes to sharp daggers of disgust.

He would deserve it. He disgusted himself!

'Zoe—' His fingers tightened around hers. She returned the pressure, her eyes vulnerable with trust. He didn't deserve her trust! And he was about to shatter it. 'It was your first time. Forgive me—I was angry— I thought—'

'I know what you thought.' One hand was tugged from his grasp, a finger laid across his mouth, effectively stopping his words because his breath went as he fought the temptation to take that soft warm finger into his mouth and start everything all over again. 'You thought Oliver Sherman and I had been lovers. I can't blame you,' she absolved him softly. 'That note he sent with those flowers,' she reminded gently. 'And when you asked me, before we married, if I'd been sleeping with him I refused to give you a straight answer.'

Her eyes glimmered, her thick lashes flickering down as she remembered her bolshie need at that time to pay him back for the double standards that told him it was OK for him to share his bed with the woman of the moment while she was expected to be chaste as a nun.

The frown line between his smoky eyes deepened. Repentant, she released her other hand and stroked it away. The movement brought her body into closer,

more intimate contact with his. She felt a long shudder rake through him and told him, 'Last night wasn't
what you thought it was. Oliver wasn't at the ceremony, I checked. He turned up at the wedding party
late on and seemed to latch onto a group of people
I'd never seen before. It was a relief. I didn't want
anything to do with him, not after that note. I was
about to leave when he jumped me. He was drunk as
a skunk, that's the only excuse I can think of—'

'There is no excuse for that kind of behaviour,'
Javier shot in tightly. No excuse for his, either.
Feeling worse than bad about himself, he stated
heavily, 'You were a virgin. I was angry, I took advantage, I'm no better than he is. You should have
told me.'

Her lips curved in a smile that turned his heart inside out. 'I could have done, and asked you to be
gentle with me—like a properly brought-up virgin
should!' An entrancing dimple told him she was up
to her old witchery. 'But I wanted you to find out for
yourself.'

'Minx!' He meant it. She wriggled against him. His
body wanted to take what she was offering. This
woman, this flirt, was twisting him around her little
finger.

This woman. His wife!

'This changes everything.' His body throbbed with
desire, but his mind took charge as he levered himself
away from the little witch and swung his legs out of
the innocent-seeming, pristine bed that had become a
honey-trap.

By making love with her he had changed the rules

that had governed their sham marriage. 'Last night you told me our marriage was over. Now I'm telling you that it isn't.' Still sitting, he reached for the shirt so hurriedly discarded the night before, shrugged into it. 'There's no question of a divorce.'

Zoe squirmed to her knees. He sounded as if he were handing out a life sentence when he was giving her paradise, everything she'd dreamed of since she was fifteen years old! Her hands slid beneath the hem of his shirt, caressing the firm warm flesh, laying her cheek against the hard span of his shoulder blade as he dragged in a harsh intake of breath.

'That's OK,' she murmured. She loved him so much she felt as if every inch of her were disintegrating, melting into a treacly river of desire and adoration. Her hands slithered round his taut body. The muscles below his ribcage were rigid, she lovingly discovered. 'You never know, I might be pregnant,' she said in a small voice, her vocal cords knotting up, all of her mind wonderingly focussed on the tightness of her breasts, the pulsating heat deep in the place that seemed to have taken centre stage in her being.

Pregnant!

Tension locked Javier's jaws together. He leapt to his feet, reaching for the remainder of his clothes, getting into them while she just flopped back against the heaped pillows and lay there, butter-wouldn't-melt, all elegant silky limbs, pale hair fanned out against the pillow, watching him with those come-bed-me eyes.

He hadn't thought. He hadn't damn well thought of anything but his driving need to claim what was his by right, the heaven he'd stoically denied himself for so long! The dam had finally burst and he'd tumbled mindlessly with the flow. And if his opinion had been asked at the start of it he'd have probably said that the 'goer' had to be well protected.

Having his back to her successfully hid his sharp wince of shattering self-loathing. Irresponsibly, he might have fathered a child. And for all he knew she might not even want to think about motherhood for several years. Was the possibility that he might have selfishly impregnated her the only reason she'd given in and changed her mind about leaving him?

And if the pregnancy scare proved to be unfounded, would she change her mind right back again and walk out on him as last night she'd unequivocally stated that she fully intended to?

Unwilling right now to inspect how he'd feel in that eventuality, Javier tightened his jaw and bit out, 'I'll see you at breakfast.' He reached the door in rapid strides, adding heavily, 'We need to talk things out fully and clear-headedly—away from your bed. Without sex to muddy the waters.'

His grim tone shook her rigid, closing up her throat. And what he'd said—did he still, in the privacy of his thoughts, name her as a whore by inclination? Her uninhibited behaviour last night, the way she'd given him unlimited access to her body, encouraging him every inch of the way, would have hammered that impression all the way home.

She stared at the door he had just closed behind him, tears welling in her eyes. The glittering prize, her acceptance as his true wife, her place in his life as the mother of the children she desperately hoped to give him turned into a handful of ashes, slipping through her fingers.

She shouldn't have mentioned the possibility of pregnancy. It had been a flip, thoughtless comment, tossed out to cover the fact that she'd been over the moon and practically speechless with happiness when he'd so strongly vetoed divorce.

He might have lusted after her, enjoyed the sex, but he wasn't in love with her, not yet, she knew that. And he would hate the responsibility if she'd come out with the truth and confessed that she'd always loved him and always would.

He took his responsibilities seriously, he was that kind of man—as evidenced by the way he'd suggested a paper marriage in the first place—so she couldn't land that on him, she decided miserably, forcing herself to leave the bed where she'd been so ecstatically happy, so hopeful about the wonderful future she and Javier would have together, so confident that she could in time teach him to love her as much as he'd learned to want her.

Clarity came when she turned off the shower and huddled into a towel. He hadn't ruled a divorce out of play because he wanted her permanently in his life—he was simply sticking to his original dateline.

Two years. They'd stay married for one more year, until she came into her inheritance and could demonstrate that she was mature enough to handle it. By his own admission he was deeply ashamed of having made love to her. No—having had sex with her—'muddied the waters', she corrected dully as she finally exited the *en suite*. And he'd probably make damn sure it didn't happen again. He'd go back to what he had been: remote, often absent, impersonally kind. She simply didn't think she could bear that!

Was she the last woman on earth he would choose to be the mother of his children? Had he seen the steel jaws of a trap close around him when she'd mentioned the word 'pregnant'?

Her balloon well and truly pricked, Zoe put on the act of her life and went down to breakfast wearing a tiny pair of lemon yellow shorts, a skimpy, silky camisole top in a matching shade and a great big smile.

Javier laid aside the morning broadsheet he'd been trying and failing to concentrate on, his wide chest tightening as his eyes locked onto his wife. She was exquisite; she put the sunlight that streamed into the room to shame. A truly vital presence, all silky, endless legs, shining silver-gilt hair, breasts enticingly peaked against the top she was wearing.

He got to his feet, narrowed eyes watching as she returned Boysie's ecstatic greeting, pulling out a chair for her when those long legs brought her to the breakfast table. She was wearing hot pink lipstick on those lush, kiss-swollen lips. His pulses quickened. He ignored them and poured her coffee.

'Eat something,' he ordered as the slice of toast she'd buttered was being cut into small pieces and fed to the dog. Had her appetite deserted her because she was fretting over the possibility of an unwanted pregnancy?

Again he mentally flayed himself. He had hated the things Sherman had implied, but hated himself even more for having been unable to stop believing them. Which had led, in turn, to his inexcusable lack of protection.

'We need to discuss our situation.' Self-disgust put an edge on his voice, made her soft lips tremble before she clamped them forcibly together. She fed the last of the toast to the tail-thrashing bunch of fur then turned to face him, pushing her hair away from her face with the back of a slender hand, her magnificent eyes flashing with the old rebellion, the slender bones of her shoulders tense beneath the shimmery fabric of the top she was wearing.

He sounded as if he thoroughly regretted their 'situation', as he so grimly named it, Zoe decided sinkingly. It was truly terrible to love to distraction when the object of all that emotional passion didn't love you back, to have all your hopes of happiness and fulfilment dependent on just one man.

But she wasn't going to let him know what she was feeling. Still holding his silver-smoke eyes, she lifted her chin even higher just as Joe entered the room, grinning. 'Pardon me, boss, but it's time for his lordship's morning walk. We usually go up through the woods and on down to the lake.' He gave a low whistle and Boysie pricked up his ears and raced to the man in the doorway, his small body one huge hairy wag.

'I'll take him—' Zoe was half out of her seat, unreasonable jealousy that her dog now recognised Joe as the leader of the pack making her voice shrill.

But Javier's hand reached out to clamp around her

wrist, forcing her back, his, 'Carry on, Joe,' full of raw impatience.

Rubbing her released wrist, Zoe glared at him, trying not to burst into tears. Not because of Boysie's fickleness—if she was honest with herself she was glad the little stray had finally integrated into his new home and family. It had taken ages before he had stopped viewing Ethel with suspicion and even longer before he had been comfortable around Joe.

No, it was Javier's attitude that was breaking her heart. Last night she had felt as if they had at last found each other, their hearts and souls recognising each other just as their bodies had, and this morning it would seem that he wished he'd never set eyes on her!

'I always take him for walks. That's when you bother to turn up to bring me down here at weekends!' Zoe knew she sounded petulant and childish. But she had to say something to explain away the sudden tears she could feel filling up her eyes. No way was she about to let him know that his patently obvious impatience with her and their cataclysmic unplanned change of marital situation was making her want to cry her eyes out!

Javier leaned forward, his forearms on the table, a frown scoring a deep line between his slashing black brows. Judging by her reaction to her pet's preference for Joe's company, the poor kid was still needy, clinging onto love wherever she found it. 'Let it go,' he advised a touch more curtly than he'd intended before the image of how unchildlike she'd been in his arms last night had flashed across his brain and made his voice emerge like a shot from a gun.

She was no kid—hadn't he known that for months now? She was all woman. It had been her first time but she'd been a natural. He went hot just thinking about it. And not with shame, either.

Shifting edgily in his seat, he told her, 'Don't be so intense about your feelings. They're likely to rear up and slap you in the face. More coffee?'

Zoe mutely shook her head. That was a warning, wasn't it? Telling her not to read too much into what had happened last night, not to take it seriously.

He looked into her glittering golden eyes, eyes to drown in, and the air in the sunny room was suddenly thick with sexual tension. She was so lovely. And she was his. It hadn't been planned, in fact he'd fought what she'd been doing to him as soon as he'd recognised it for what it was.

But what the hell? Their sham marriage had turned into vivid reality and he aimed to keep it that way. He would concentrate all his powers to make her forget she'd ever decided to walk away from him.

The probably pompous discussion about their altered relationship was promptly jettisoned.

What kind of fool had he been to think he could keep this beautiful, slightly elusive, bright and feisty creature by spouting a list of ground rules?

A fool who hadn't recognised the fact that he'd been falling in love, hook, line and sinker.

But it was too soon to let her know that. She might have believed herself to be in love with him at age sixteen. An adolescent infatuation she'd grown out of.

Must have done or she wouldn't have been determined to walk out on him.

He'd reel her in gently. Make sure she didn't want to live without him.

Leaning back in his chair, he relaxed utterly. He felt as though a heavy weight had been lifted from his shoulders. He always got what he wanted in the end. He made it happen. His mouth curved in a dazzling smile.

As always Zoe drowned in the smile that had been absent for far too long, her body filling with primal need as the fluid grace with which he leaned back in his chair reinforced the myriad reasons she loved this man. And when he turned the shameless magic of his grin on her again and told her, 'We fly out to Spain next week for a belated honeymoon,' her wits scattered to the four corners of the room and she could only stare back at him, her cheeks reddening with pleasure, her mind in a muddle because she would never understand what was going on in his head from one minute to the next.

But trying to find out would be exciting!

CHAPTER SIX

THE Spanish sun blazed down and the aquamarine sea glittered back at it with improbable intensity. The leaves of the overhanging eucalyptus tree moved with silvery languour in the slight, soft breeze.

Zoe turned from staring down unseeingly at the tranquil view of the deserted sandy beach beyond the manicured gardens. Her lush mouth compressed into a tight line, she leant back against the ornate stone balustrade that surrounded the terrace that ran round three sides of the white-walled Moorish-style villa, her heart jumping beneath her breastbone as Javier emerged through an archway, a tray of cold drinks in his strong hands.

He'd changed from the clothes he'd travelled in. Just looking at him made her feel light-headed. Her wretched mouth began to wobble again as her eyes drank in his spectacular male body clad now in casual shorts that hung low on his lean hips, and a white T-shirt that did wonders for his sleek olive-toned skin and lovingly clung to his impressive torso.

The muscles guarding her sex quivered and her breath locked tight in her lungs. They were here together in this beautiful, romantic spot but they might as well be on different planets. Utterly disorientated because of his unfathomable attitude towards her since the night they'd made love, Zoe didn't know whether she wanted to laugh or to cry. It would be far too easy to do both at once.

Biting down on her soft lower lip to stop herself doing either, or more probably both, she forced herself to walk slowly down the length of the long terrace to the table in the shade of a vine where he was placing what appeared to be a frosted jug of juice and two tall glasses.

Everything had happened so quickly and that was part of the trouble, she thought edgily. When Javier decided on a course of action he didn't hang about.

Initially, she'd thought his mention of a honeymoon meant that they were to embark on a real and lasting marriage, cancelling out her earlier fear that he would be sticking to his original time-span of their empty marriage, making sure the mistake of the night before was never repeated.

Provided, of course, that she wasn't pregnant.

If she was then, being an honourable man, he would bite the bullet and resign himself to his fate. An impossible scenario. It made her feel physically ill just to think about it.

So the way he'd smiled at her and mentioned a belated honeymoon had made her deliriously happy, confident that after the magic of what had happened between them the night before he wanted her permanently in his life, was already halfway to falling in love with her. But that state of euphoria had lasted for a couple of hours only.

Because now she wasn't so sure.

She wasn't sure at all.

'I wondered where you had got to.' He looked at

her and smiled that bone-weakening smile of his. A lock of his soft dark hair had fallen over his forehead. Her fingers itched to run through it, push it back into place.

She sat down instead, watched him take the chair opposite and shrugged lightly. 'I wanted to get my bearings.' Wanted to snatch a slice of time by herself would be nearer the truth, to try to figure out what was going on inside that clever head of his, what he truly wanted of her, of their marriage.

That other morning at breakfast, two minutes after telling her they would be heading for a belated honeymoon at his parents' winter home in Spain, he'd shut himself in the technological wonder that was his Wakeham Lodge study, emerging a couple of hours later to drive himself back to London, only sparing her the time to impart in the clinical tone she dreaded, 'I'll be back to collect you in a couple of days. I'll pick up our passports from the apartment and pack for us both.' Not even a goodbye kiss. Hardly lover-like behaviour. Right then all her hopeful happiness had taken a sharp nosedive.

'You've been here before, remember?' he reminded as he set a glass of juice down in front of her.

There was a knowing light in those smoky, heavily fringed eyes. Was he laughing at her? Mocking?

Of course she remembered! How could she forget the way she'd humiliated herself? That passionate declaration of love—he hadn't wanted her love then and it looked as if he didn't want it now.

She offered a languid shrug. Two could be cool

and uninterested. 'So? It's been, what, three years? A long time, anyway. Things change.'

But she hadn't changed. She still loved him to absolute distraction. And he hadn't, either. He still saw her as a tiresome responsibility, especially after the night he obviously preferred to forget and wholeheartedly wished had never happened.

Zoe's fingers closed round the ice-cold surface of the glass. When he'd collected her from Wakeham Lodge early this morning he'd been back to being polite but distant. And flying over on the company jet she had spikily wondered if there were any other couple in the history of the world, embarking on their honeymoon who weren't at least holding hands!

And every time she'd tried to talk about what was really important, such as how he saw their future, he'd smoothly changed the subject and stuck his nose back into the file of documents that had been waiting for him when they'd boarded. So she'd given up.

But now: 'How long will we be here?' Zoe connected with his stunning eyes, held his smoky gaze and tried to look as if her question weren't all that important, just idle conversation. But it was something that had been really muddling her. From his attitude—back to the status quo—she was growing surer with each hour that passed that the no-divorce thing he'd insisted on applied only to the next year.

He stuck like a limpet to what he saw as his duty. Over the years she had learned that it was an intrinsic part of his strong, macho character. So why bother to bring her out here to Almeria, to this isolated spot a few kilometres from the tiny unspoiled village of La

Isleta del Moro? From her perspective it didn't make a whole lot of sense.

Not to make mad passionate love to her, really cement their marriage, that was for sure. He hadn't so much as touched her in passing since that night.

And not to broaden her horizons, either, although in the back of the chauffeur-driven car that had met them at the airport he had, very politely, given her the tourist spiel: the rugged province of Almeria was the hottest and driest in Spain, the mild winter temperatures made it ideal for his parents when the winter closed in over the mountains. The spaghetti westerns had been filmed here—on and on until, frustrated and heart-wrenchingly miserable over the complete lack of anything remotely personal coming from his direction, she'd wanted to smack his face.

Now, looking into that same breathtakingly handsome face, she waited, more wired-up with each passing second. He had some explaining to do!

'As long as it takes,' Javier unthinkingly answered, watching the tiny pulse beat at the base of her long, elegant neck, following the tense line of her delicate collar-bones, and down to the warm honey skin revealed by the open-necked silk shirt she was wearing.

She was tense, wary, taut as a bowstring, the light in those magnificent golden eyes partly suspicion, partly defiance. The urge to take her in his arms and hold her tight was hard to resist.

Javier smothered a sigh. He had to be patient, tread very carefully. He knew the way her mind worked. One hint of pressure and she'd be off at the speed of light. Three days ago she'd been ready to run. She would have had her reasons. He doubted that one night of sex would have changed them. But she was his and he was determined to keep her. So play it cool and play it slow, take as much time as needed to bind her to him for all time—

'As long as it takes to find out if you've got me pregnant!' she flashed out as she scrambled to her feet. She had the answer to her question now and she didn't like it one little bit! She slapped away the outstretched hand that would have stayed her, and her long legs took her flying for the sanctuary of the villa.

She had suspected as much, hadn't she? So why did it hurt so much? Why should she feel traumatised and shocked when he came out with the truth?

The cool ambience of the villa's interior, all white marble floors, watery green colour-washed walls, elegant classic furnishings, did nothing to soothe her tumultuous emotions.

Had he reverted to the part of a polite stranger to hide the fact that he was sick to his stomach thinking about what—honour-bound—he'd have to do if she proved to be carrying his child? Stick by her for the rest of his life, give up the bachelor freedom he relished and had still felt free to follow during the latter part of their paper marriage?

'You'll want to freshen up after the journey. I'll show you to our room.'

Zoe all but leapt out of her skin. She hadn't heard him follow her inside. Heart thumping wildly, she decided she hated him. Really and utterly!

'Don't bother.' Her voice was nicely chilling she

noted with empty satisfaction. 'Teresa can show me where I'm to sleep.'

She perfectly remembered the round, smiley señora from her previous stay here. Full-time housekeeper when Javier's parents or guests were in residence. She wished Teresa would appear right now, or her husband, Manuel, who seemed to have disappeared entirely since he'd delivered them here from the airport.

Someone—anyone—to act as a buffer between her and Javier, the husband who didn't want her, who almost certainly regarded what had happened between them as a deeply regrettable one-night stand and shuddered every time he thought about it.

But his firm hand beneath her elbow was guiding her to the foot of the sweeping marble staircase with its delicate iron-work bannisters and he was telling her, 'On my instructions Teresa's gone back to her home in the village. Manuel, too. Honeymooning couples need to be alone, wouldn't you say?'

Zoe tripped over her own feet as the breath whooshed out of her lungs at that cynical statement. This honeymooning couple needed to be alone so that the hired staff wouldn't be tempted to gossip about how unloverlike they actually were!

Misery and shame overwhelmed her. If she hadn't enthusiastically encouraged him to bed her they wouldn't be in this weird situation! And she wouldn't have to be pretending that she could take it in her stride when in reality she felt as if her heart were shattering.

Suddenly, the elegant staircase looked like a sheer cliff face. Zoe's buckled knees began to shake.

Shooting her an amused look from heavily veiled smoky eyes, Javier swept her up into his arms before she could fully collect herself and carried her up the stairs with no effort at all, tutting mildly when she squirmed and huffed, 'Put me down!' as they approached the open arched doorway of the magnificent master bedroom.

'It's tradition. The groom carries his bride over the threshold.'

Desperately trying not to let her body's instinctive response to his reveal itself as he slowly slid her down his impressive length and settled her prone upon the bed, she immediately came back with a raspingly breathless, 'There's no one around to applaud your performance, so you needn't have risked a hernia!'

She was wallowing in the fallout of her own shame. That night had been so special to her, just a horrendous mistake as far as he was concerned. And as if to emphasise that embarrassing fact he stepped smartly back from the bed as if he didn't want to be anywhere near her.

Scrambling into a sitting position—no way was she just going to lie where he'd put her, like an invitation he would never dream of accepting, ever again—she pouted. 'In case you'd forgotten, we've been married for almost a year, so I'm hardly a ''bride''. So all that carrying over the threshold is just a sick joke. You never carried me over anything before.'

A sick, hurtful joke, a mockery of everything she'd hoped this marriage would be. Tears stung at the backs of her eyes. She willed them not to fall and swallowed convulsively, her head downbent, her fingers knotted together, her poor heart getting another mangling when Javier mused softly, 'I remember what must have been the last time I carried you. You were ten years old and had spent an entire Sunday racing around the zoo, trying to see everything at once. You were too tired to make it back to the car. You fell instantly asleep in my arms. It was as if someone had switched you off. I remember thinking what a cute scrap you were, in spite of those long, gawky legs and dirty little face!'

He backed off doorwards, clipped practicality to the fore, as if he was wondering where that soppy memory had come from. 'Have a shower and a nap. Teresa unpacked for you so you'll find your gear in the dressing room. We'll have a late supper.' Leaving her to remember how the seeds for an adult love had been sown in the child she had been in the days when he had been like a big brother, caring and kind, the nicest, most wonderful person she knew.

Slotting the arched wood into the doorframe with exaggerated care, Javier gritted his teeth and pulled a long hiss of breath into his lungs. It had been a close-run thing. He only had to look at her to want her, his body threatening to take control and blow his cerebral plans to smithereens.

When he'd made love to her from the starting point of the possessive anger he'd not known he was re-motely capable of he'd experienced the most mind-blowing event of his life. She'd been spectacular, a fast and eager learner. He knew he would only have to go back into that room and take her in his arms, kiss her, to instigate the repeat performance his whole body was aching for.

Even now the temptation to stride straight back into the bedroom was eating into his brain like acid, slyly telling him that she was his wife, that they'd already made love, that she'd proved beyond all possible doubt that she was highly sexed and passionate, and that denying himself another slice of that heaven was a ridiculous sacrifice.

But something else had happened that night, hadn't it? He stalked towards the stairs, through the house, out to the swimming pool, dragging his T-shirt over his head as he went.

Love had happened. It might have slammed into his brain like a sledgehammer at the time but with sober hindsight he recognised that it had been growing for over a year.

Shedding his shorts, he dived into the cool green waters, his lean, powerful muscles taut with frustration. Throughout the long years he had known Zoe she had engendered every emotion known to man. Delight, exasperation, compassion, caring, anger, possessive jealousy. And now love, the mother and father of all emotions. Love, deep, passionate and unblinkered. He knew her faults—that she could be headstrong and stubborn—and he knew her strong points, her liveliness and generosity of spirit. The way she walked, the way she smiled—he adored everything about her. For the first time in his life he was totally and irredeemably hooked.

His jawline grim, he powered through the water, burning all that edgy energy, scornful now of his po-faced, blinkered behaviour when he'd so nobly decided to propose an unconsummated marriage to keep her out of the clutches of the likes of Sherman. Not allowing himself to acknowledge that he'd wanted her for himself because he'd been in love with her.

Prat!

Now he was stuck between a rock and a hard place. Wanting to take that beautiful face between his hands and kiss that lush mouth until she quivered with wanton anticipation, peel the clothes from her lovely body and pleasure her until they were both damn near expiring from sexual overload.

But knowing that he mustn't. Couldn't. Shouldn't. He had never had any trouble getting any woman he wanted—in fact he'd perfected the knack of fighting them off, and that, instead of stoking his ego, had begun to bore him.

Zoe was different. He was diving deeper and deeper in love with her with every passing second. He had to teach her to love him back, to want to spend the rest of her life with him, have his children—

He groaned, increased the pace of his furious strokes, churning the erstwhile placid water. His selfishness appalled him. What he wanted shouldn't be the main issue here, not while his poor darling was worrying herself silly over the possibility of pregnancy.

She had a whole lot of living to do before she settled down to the responsibility of motherhood and he knew she was troubled and edgily anxious. Hadn't he witnessed her reaction, the way she'd snapped and brought up the troubled subject when in answer to her question he'd replied, 'As long as it takes.' Meaning, of course, that the length of their stay here was dependent on the time it took for him to make her love him just half as much as he adored her.

Trouble was, he conceded heavily, no one could make Zoe do anything she didn't want to do.

The rock and the hard place expanded to massive proportions.

Edgy, Zoe couldn't settle. And as for taking a nap as Javier had so coolly suggested, it was completely out of the question.

Opting for the huge sunken bath in the spacious *en suite* as likely to be potentially more relaxing than the power shower, she'd lain in the perfumed hot water staring at the creamy marble walls, the glass shelves bearing expensive essences and lotions, the shiny green leaves of the potted plants, for around five minutes until her fraught emotions had driven her right out again.

What was Javier doing?

That he was here, somewhere around, but she couldn't see or hear him, spooked her. He was a workaholic, she knew that. And she'd seen the bulging briefcase and the laptop, part of the copious luggage he deemed necessary for their stay.

So he was probably in one or other of the air-conditioned sitting rooms, totally absorbed in some structural engineering project, while she was beating herself up over the unresolved situation they found themselves in. Man-like, he would be able to put it out of his mind, not wasting mental energy on a problem that couldn't be solved until they knew whether or not she was pregnant.

Despising herself for being unable to do likewise, she entered the dressing room to find something to wear. Vast fitted hanging cupboards, two chests of drawers, an antique pier-glass.

Teresa had unpacked for her, so he'd told her. He'd also said 'our room', she remembered. The fine line of her arched brows drew together as her heart began a foolish gallop. Was he really expecting them to share a room, a bed?

Get real, she told herself forcefully before she could get too excited by that prospect and what it might mean. Teresa's unpacking all their gear in the shared room would have been proposed to nip gossip in the bud, as had his decision to tell her and Manuel that their services would not be needed. The true state of their marriage had been kept from his parents, so he would want to guard against the likelihood of Teresa confiding in his mother that her son and daughter-in-law didn't sleep together.

She dismissed that miserable thought. A rapid inspection revealed that the hanging cupboard on one side of the room contained just about every lightweight garment she owned, and a row of his stuff in the other—ranging from smart-casual right down to knockabout washed-out jeans and cut-offs.

Very His and Hers.

So, OK. He'd use the dressing room. But he would have no desire to share her bed. He'd use one of the others. You bet he would! Hadn't he demonstrated that he had no wish to get any closer to her than inhabiting the same slab of the planet necessitated?

Snatching a turquoise silk wrap from the depths of the space allotted to her, she thrust her arms into it and savagely tied the sash around her waist. Javier was hateful! She didn't know why she loved the brute! Didn't he realise that she had feelings?

The brute who was filling her head to the exclusion of anything else appeared in the dressing-room doorway. Zoe felt his presence, so immediate and compelling, like a blow to her solar plexus and spun round to face him, the fine silk of her wrap clinging to her still-damp body.

Her face flushed feverishly. He was utterly, unfairly gorgeous, wearing just those low-slung shorts, his skin slicked with water, his dark hair clinging to his skull. And just for a moment she saw tension grip that sensational bone structure, his eyes narrowing as if to block out the unwelcome sight of her. And then it was gone, the beginnings of a politely impersonal, meaningless smile starting to deal with the savage line of his mouth.

And before he could come out with an equally meaningless pseudo pleasantry Zoe got a grip, not willing to let him guess how this game of manners was winding her up to the point of explosion. 'You've been swimming,' she cooed. 'What a great idea!' She bounced to the Hers chest of drawers, breathed a short but heartfelt sigh of gratitude as her hand fell on her favourite bikini.

Clutching it to her heaving breasts, she sped from

the room at a speed that ensured she was able to keep an empty smile on her face before it could inevitably crumple into stifled sobs as soon as she hit the privacy of the outer corridor.

CHAPTER SEVEN

AS USUAL Javier woke early, snapping awake as if he'd been plugged into a power circuit. His mind homing straight in on Zoe asleep in the master suite on the other side of the villa.

During the five days they'd been here he'd got exactly nowhere with his too-confident plan to softly persuade her to start believing that they could have a good life together, the best. He'd actually gone backwards, in his puzzled estimation. Of the Zoe he knew and had grown to love—the talkative, perky, sometimes stroppy, always vital, generous, intriguing minx he had known for most of her life—there had been no sign.

His ego-driven decision to make her change her mind about walking away from their marriage— showing her what a real nice guy he was, considerate and caring of her, undemanding and smothering his natural inclination to call all the shots, demonstrating that making love to her wasn't the first and only thing on his agenda and hopefully rekindling something of her earlier, self-confessed love for him—wasn't working. So he would have to jettison that approach and go for a more open strategy.

No matter how hard he'd tried to make her time here in Spain with him a truly enjoyable experience he'd come up against a solid brick wall. Every outing or new experience he'd suggested had been met with downswept eyes and a mute shake of her beautiful spun-gold head.

Once he'd made his mind up on a plan of action he always carried it through. This time it had backfired on him big time. She spent most of her waking time in the little summerhouse deep in the garden, her pretty nose buried in a book, and all his attempts to discover what was troubling her—for something obviously was—had been met with a stubborn, 'Nothing'. He wasn't used to being thwarted. His dark brows thundered together as he contemplated this new experience.

Under the cold shower, one of the many he'd been forced to take while he'd been pussyfooting around the woman who only had to walk into the room to have his craving body leap to attention, he decided grimly that this unbearable stand-off had to end.

In the past Zoe had always been able to talk to him, about anything and everything, and he remembered with yet another shock that he disliked chattering women but that with Zoe it had always been different. He'd relished every word she'd ever said to him. If it was the last thing he did in this life he would get her confiding in him again, opening up about what was wrong with her.

It came to him as he pulled on a pair of denim cutoffs that she might actually be ill. The thought terrified him into snatching up a sleeveless T-shirt and dragging it over his head at speed.

No one could deny that there were dark shadows around those lovely eyes, a worrying pallor lying over her tense features and her normal healthy appetite had shrunk out of existence.

Javier had never felt distraught in the whole of his life and he was trying to deal with that unwelcome emotion when the thought that the reason for her withdrawal and unwell appearance could be down to worry struck him with the force of a runaway ten-ton truck.

Her fear of possible pregnancy!

His intention to make coffee and take a cup to her room forgotten, he froze on his feet at the foot of the staircase he'd descended at foolhardy speed.

All his fault.

She'd been all set to cut loose—she'd stated that all too clearly—leave him behind while she made her own life, found her own friends, and now she would be afraid that an unwelcome pregnancy would shatter all her plans for single-woman freedom.

Snapping around, Javier hared back up the stairs, taking them two at a time. Convinced he now knew what her un-Zoe-like behaviour signified, he had the solution. He had to reassure her, remove all her fears and worries at a single stroke.

No question of the divorce she'd said she wanted, of course, that went without saying, but she had to know that if she was carrying his child she would have nothing to worry about. She would get the very best ongoing gynaecological attention that money could buy, and he, personally, would wrap her in cotton wool, cherish her, and the baby when he or she arrived would never know a moment's neglect if she wanted to pursue her voluntary charity work because top-notch professional nannies would be employed around the clock.

Besides, he thought with a rush of warmth to the region of his heart, he would enjoy the experience of parenting and would take to it like a duck to water.

But whatever his wishes on that subject, Zoe came first and always would and she had to know that. He could not, would not, stand by, say nothing, while he watched her worry herself half to death!

As Zoe climbed out of the bath and wrapped a towel around her body she knew she had to tell Javier and put his mind at rest.

Today. She could delay it no longer. Keeping the news to herself for five whole days was desperately unfair; she knew that, and didn't much like herself for such uncharacteristic sneakiness.

Catching sight of her miserably guilty face in the mirror, she looked away quickly. Black bags under her eyes and a complexion the shade of putty she did not want to have to see.

These last days had been torment. Javier had been at his kindest, astonishingly patient and gently affectionate, never seeming to mind when she turned down his invitations to go swimming, sailing, eating at a quayside restaurant where, he told her, the speciality lobster dish was out of this world.

And her eyes actually swam with tears when she recalled his gentleness when he'd asked her if anything was troubling her. The unhidden concern in those smoky eyes had made her heart ache.

She'd almost blurted the truth out then but the arrival of Teresa with the daily fresh provisions, the only few minutes of contact Javier allowed the housekeeper with the so-called honeymooning couple, had stopped her.

There wasn't going to be a baby.

She'd known that since their first night here. And kept it to herself because her feelings were so horrendously mixed up she didn't know what they actually were.

On the one hand she had secretly longed to have Javier's baby and finding out that she wasn't going to had been a source of really surprisingly deep regret. Yet if she had been pregnant she knew that he would have insisted that they stay married for the sake of their child, and not because he was madly in love with her and wanted her in his life for ever.

Heck no, she knew how his mind worked. He would grit his teeth and do his duty and she wouldn't have been able to bear the thought that she was an unwelcome albatross around his neck.

And once she told him he could forget the pregnancy scare he would breathe one huge sigh of relief and the status quo would be firmly back in place. And in less than a year, just as soon as she reached her majority and he deemed her fit to handle her huge inheritance, he would consider his duty done and be off out of their marriage at the speed of light, gratefully embracing his new-found bachelor freedom.

Little wonder she was muddled, riven by mixed feelings and terminally depressed.

The moment she was dressed she would find him and confess her sins of omission and have to watch the grin of relief light up his lean and handsome features and know that her mission to get him to fall in love with her had been a complete failure, all her fond hopes vanishing without a trace.

Hopes that had taken a steep nosedive when his behaviour had turned so distant after the night of love-making he had to have considered to be a reprehensible mistake because he had shown absolutely no desire for a repeat performance; hopes that had wriggled their deceiving way into her muddled head during the past few days when he had been so kind.

But 'kind' she could do without. It harked right back to his treatment of her during her childhood. A full-grown woman now, she needed more. Much more. And he was patently unwilling to give it.

As she walked out of the bathroom, feeling as if she were about to face a firing squad, the main door to the suite opened with a decisive swing and the love of her life stood there, determination written all over his hard bone structure.

Panic brought her heart jumping up into her throat. As always his sensational looks made her mouth run dry. Clutching at the edges of the slipping bath towel and before her courage deserted her she pushed out a bald, 'I'm not pregnant.'

For a moment Javier looked poleaxed, his eyes darkening, and it wasn't a flicker of disappointment she saw there, of course it wasn't because in the next split second a warm smile was irradiating his unforgettable features.

A smile of wholehearted relief, she decided sickly. He would not now be called upon to do his duty. In a little under a year's time he would sling his hook, smugly congratulating himself that as far as her well-being was concerned he had done everything that could be expected of him.

The depth of his disappointment shocked Javier for the few moments it took to remind himself he was being utterly selfish. He might want to see her hold his child in her arms, but worrying about the possibility had been making her ill. He had to think of how relieved she must be feeling and not dwell on his own disappointment.

He made himself smile and advanced a step towards the tense little darling, all wrapped up in a towel like a parcel waiting to be opened, her silvery gold hair tumbling in enchanting disarray around her naked shoulders. His voice sounded strangely roughened as he told her warmly, 'Then from now on you can stop worrying. I know you have been.'

He knew nothing! Patronising hog!

'I've known for a good five days, so don't pretend you can read my mind!' she flung at him in temper, thoroughly hating him for that grin of utter relief at being let off the hook that his pride and his honour would have had him impaled on for the rest of his life.

And hating herself even more for immediately bursting into a torrent of tears and giving way to out-of-control sobs when his strong arms enfolded her, one gentle hand pressing her head against the accommodating wide span of his shoulder.

'Hush, sweetheart. I can't bear to see you cry! It really cuts me up,' Javier uttered on a driven undertone and Zoe felt she had been somehow swept back over a decade in time. Wrenching her head away from what she didn't want to admit to being the comfort of his solid shoulder, she flailed her small fists against the immovable barrier of his chest.

'I'm not an eight-year-old kid any more!' she bit out in raw-edged fury. 'So don't treat me like one! Next thing you'll be saying, ''There there'' and promising to buy me an ice cream if I wipe my eyes and blow my nose!' Breasts heaving with emotion, tear-drenched eyes flashing fire in his direction, Zoe ranted at him. She knew she was being unfair. Few men would enjoy the spectacle of a woman turning on the waterworks, and he'd only been trying to make her stop blubbering. But that knowledge didn't prevent her from renewing her assault on that broad chest and doing her damnedest to put space between them.

But Javier simply hauled her closer to the lean, hard strength of his body, amusement curling that wide, sensual mouth, his voice dark and drawly. 'Should I also go the whole hog and offer to kiss you better?'

Zoe's heart gave a violent lurch. Her wide eyes met the suddenly smouldering intensity of his and her mouth ran dry. A tiny quiver assailed her as she felt her skin tighten. His mouth promised passion. Her own lips softened, parting on a slight tremor as the hands that had been holding her captive became instruments of exquisite torture as they slid up to splay against the naked skin of her shoulder blades. Her head began to spin and she thought she heard herself moan as the aggression melted out of her fisted hands and her palms flattened over the soft fabric of his T-shirt and registered the rapid beat of his heart.

And then that perfect, intoxicatingly sexy male mouth descended to take hers and fireworks exploded inside the entirety of Zoe's being. Her slim arms lifted to twine around his neck and the towel slipped to the floor and this time the driven groan came from him as his hands travelled down the line of her spine, settled with male possessiveness on her hips and curved her against his hard body.

Zoe's fingers tangled in the luxuriance of his thick black hair as the mastery of his mouth sent her spinning to heaven, too dizzy and disorientated to take in what he was saying when his mouth parted from hers and he asked on a thickened undertone, 'Is this what you want? You have to be sure. Tell me now—I'm not made of stone.'

Gazing up into the breathtaking feverish glitter of his darkened eyes, Zoe missed his mouth like crazy. She wanted it back. Now. Pressing even closer, if that were possible, she claimed what she craved, drowning in euphoria as she felt the deep shudder rake its way through his honed, lean frame. as his lips ravished hers with blistering passion.

He did want her, was the exultant thought that made its way through her fogged brain. His body betrayed how much. He wasn't indifferent! With an instinct as old as Eve her hips rotated against his in out-of-control need.

'Zoe—' Sheer will-power brought his mouth from the honeyed nectar of hers, aware that his voice sounded like the rasp of an iron file. The beautiful little minx was driving him wild, everything getting way out of hand—

The hard tips of her breasts scorched through his T-shirt. His sanity was on the verge of leaving him. He brought his hands up to cup her face, his fingers sliding under the thick silver-gold hair that fell softly around her flushed face, a perfect frame for those liquid topaz eyes fringed with ridiculously long lashes, delicate cheekbones and lush, ripe lips.

He pushed her name out again, then dragged back some of his slipping sanity. 'Wait—'

'Can't!' She trembled with the tension he was racking up, turned her head to one side and kissed the palm of his hand. The need he had aroused in her when she'd thought that making love to her again was the last thing he wanted was unbearable.

But he dropped a light kiss on her parted lips, another on the point of her neat chin, then ran unsteady hands down over her almost painfully sensitised breasts, slickly over the slight curve of her tummy before coming to rest on the soft, silky curls between her thighs, making all the breath rush out of her lungs.

'I'll be two seconds,' he promised on a raw intake of air. 'I won't put you through another pregnancy scare,' he imparted. Javier took a step away, against every instinct. Had to move before he lost the ability to think straight. 'Have to protect you this time,' he told her gently as she reached out to slip her hands beneath the hem of his T-shirt, the words that were about to tumble from her tongue, telling him that she wanted his baby with all her heart and soul dying in her throat as a raised female voice cut through the heavily charged atmosphere.

Shocked into stillness, it was Javier who broke the sudden silence with a vehement oath in a language Zoe took to be Spanish, tacking on, 'My mother!'

The tap of high heels on the polished hardwood floorboards, the, 'Javier! Teresa! Is no one here?' had Zoe realising she was naked and scrambling to cover herself with the bath towel, just as the door swung open to frame Isabella Maria wearing an aqua silk two-piece and a delighted grin.

'So there you are! The place was like the *Marie Celeste*. We've come to surprise you!'

The hard flush that had stained Javier's jutting cheekbones receding, he said drily, 'Perfect timing, as usual, Mama.' He draped an arm round Zoe's shoulders and Isabella Maria, not recognising sarcasm when she heard it, broadened her smile.

'Good! Your father said we wouldn't be welcome. But I told him not to be so foolish. You're well past the honeymoon stage and likely to shoot intruders on sight! You do realise, don't you, that I haven't seen either of you for a whole year?'

'Is that so?' Javier's tone was dryer than the desert. 'If you'll excuse us, we were about to take a shower, weren't we, darling?'

At the increased pressure on her shoulder, Zoe swallowed a giggle, managed a nod, and managed not to explode with manic laughter when Javier instructed his parent, 'Make breakfast, Mama. Zoe and I enjoy fending for ourselves, but as you're here you might as well do it.'

A series of decisive strides took him to Isabella Maria's side. A hand clamped beneath her elbow, he escorted her back through the door, firmly closing it in her surprised wake.

His hands spread, he turned to Zoe, his mouth wry as he murmured drolly, 'What can I say?'

'That you ought to fix padlocks on the doors?' Zoe's smile was wobbly because rivers of frustration were rushing through her veins, making her bones ache.

But a slashing grin of amusement curved Javier's sensational mouth. 'There's a thought!' Veiled, dark-as-charcoal eyes lingered on her lush, kiss-swollen mouth. He gave himself a savage mental shake and headed to the bathroom door. 'I'll take another cold shower while you dress.'

'Javier—wait—' Towel trailing, Zoe trotted after him, determined not to linger one moment longer in this state of limbo. How did he see their future long-term? Would they still be together beyond the further year he had originally stipulated? Or not? Was he just using her for sex because he was a normal, virile male and she was more than willing and definitely available?

'We would have had sex again,' she blurted thickly, hot colour washing over her face. But he had called a temporary halt because even in the coils of steamy passion he couldn't face the thought of being trapped by the fear of an unwanted pregnancy all over again. 'We can't just pretend it didn't happen. We have to talk.'

He had gone very still. The muscles of his arm

beneath the hand that had stayed him were like rigid iron bars. As if he no longer wanted her to touch him, Zoe decided with anguish.

Noting with a sinking feeling that she'd said having sex and not making love, Javier studied her with dark, intense eyes. Her colour had receded, leaving her skin pale and translucent. She was so lovely, so loved, it made his heart ache. And so sexually responsive it blew his mind. What was she trying to imply? That sex changed nothing? That she still wanted to go? Of course they had to talk, that had always been on his agenda. But his parents' wretched surprise visit seemed to have robbed him of the time he needed.

Battening down his rage at the untimely interruption to his plans to get his wife well and truly addicted to him, he told her with forced lightness, 'We'll talk later. Tonight. That's a promise. Right now I can't ensure Mama won't come steaming back in here in a panic.'

Shuddering inside with the strength of his frustration, he managed a soft placatory kiss on her startled mouth. 'She's never had to make a meal in the whole of her pampered life. Even now she's probably trying to figure out how to make toast and will breeze back in here demanding to know why Teresa isn't doing the job she's been handsomely paid to do!'

Zoe's hand dropped from his arm as he swung away. Even now her every cell fizzed with the erotic memories of what had been happening before Isabella Maria had broken into what would appear to be sheer fantasy.

Her fantasy that sexual desire equated with love. It

didn't; it wasn't a given. Walking with a marked lack of enthusiasm into the dressing room to pick out something to wear, Zoe focussed on the way Javier had so lightly shrugged off what had happened.

He'd been going to make love to her—no, she amended, determined to call a spade a spade even if it did hurt horribly. He'd been going to have sex with her. The interruption had caused him a minor physical inconvenience. Nothing more. True, he'd promised they'd talk everything through tonight.

But Zoe wasn't at all sure she would like what he said.

CHAPTER EIGHT

'LEAVE that to me, Mama.' Javier took the cafetière from Isabella Maria's long white hands. He'd showered and dressed at the speed of light to get down before Zoe emerged. He didn't need an audience when he told his parents to hop it. 'You don't put it directly on the stove to boil.' Ruefully affectionate exasperation roughened his tone as he pointed out, 'You're worse than a two-year-old around anything that smacks remotely of domesticity!' He tipped out the cold water and, at a guess, half a pound of soggy coffee grounds, while Isabella Maria raised her eyes to the ceiling and shrugged her elegant shoulders.

'Why would I want to know my way around kitchens?' she asked without a shadow of defensiveness in her voice. 'There are people about who are paid to see to that sort of thing for me. And, in any case, why is Teresa not here?'

'I told her her services were not required beyond a daily delivery of fresh produce. Zoe and I wanted to be alone.' Javier told it as it was as the kettle boiled and he poured the hot water over the fresh coffee grounds. And if that wasn't a big enough hint then he'd lay it on with a trowel.

And Lionel Masters, hovering in the open arched doorway as he wandered in from the terrace, listening to the exchange with a barely hidden smile, put in,

'Didn't I warn you a surprise visit wouldn't be welcome?'

'My only son not welcome his mama!' Black eyes flashed scorn. A pampered, perfectly manicured hand was laid against Javier's lean bronzed cheek. 'Do not say such foolish things, husband! What are two, three days? Besides—' dark eyes held a reproachful gleam '—I have a private message for Javier, remember?'

Not waiting for Lionel's confirmation, Isabella Maria announced primly, 'I have had rabid phone calls from a former *enamorada*—Glenda Havers, she called herself. She appears to be quite desperate to see you. She tried Ethel and Joe at Wakeham, but they on your instructions apparently refused to tell her where you were. She tried your London apartment, then the staff at Head Office—but you'd told no one there where you would be, or how long you'd be away. So as a last resort she contacted me, your mama.'

Laying a dramatic hand across her silk-clad bosom, she imparted, 'Naturally, I didn't say where you were, I was most discreet. I merely—and reluctantly, I might add—promised to pass on the message.' She shook her exquisitely coiffed head disapprovingly. 'Why she should need to have contact with you so desperately and in the shortest possible time, I neither know, or wish to. The likes of that one should have been put behind you since your marriage.'

Outside the door, Zoe heard every word and her stomach curdled. She'd taken her time over choosing what to wear, wanting to look her best to help her face the rest of the day with courage. Get through the long hours before tonight when Javier would finally tell her what he wanted of her and their marriage.

That he'd been going to make love to her didn't give her the answer. He was a normal virile male, wasn't he? Why shouldn't he take advantage of his willing wife? It didn't mean he was thinking of a lifetime of devotion, stuff like that. Like a lot of men, he could enjoy sex without his emotions being involved.

Her nerves had been on edge and now they were screaming. If she'd breezed straight into the kitchen instead of dawdling reluctantly towards the source of the voices she wouldn't have overheard. They said ignorance was bliss, didn't they?

Glenda. Glenda Havers. To her knowledge the luscious brunette had stayed the course with Javier for far longer than the few weeks it took him to grow bored with a new conquest.

And not only because she had obliged him by accompanying his self-inflicted ward on the grown-up holiday treats he'd promised her?

Was Glenda Havers still special to him? Had it been her laughter she'd heard when Javier had spoken to her from his hotel room in Cannes? Had she been his close travelling companion on those increasingly regular business trips he'd taken?

And why was she so desperate to make contact with him? Because their affair was long-standing, their relationship running deep, and they couldn't bear to be out of touch with each other for longer than a day or two?

So many questions and no answers. Zoe took a

deep breath, briefly closed her eyes and swallowed convulsively. Later, she would demand those answers. But would Javier tell her the truth?

Would he tell her what she was helplessly trying not to suspect—that in a year's time, when their marriage was over and his duty was done, he would probably decide it was time to settle down and marry his mistress of many years' standing?

And would she be able to bear it?

Straightening her slender shoulders, she pinned a smile on her face and walked into the kitchen where Javier was toasting rolls and Lionel was loading a tray with china, fruit and honey ready to carry out to the table on the terrace, the activities watched over by a languid Isabella Maria.

'Zoe—how lovely you look! I wish I could wear sugar-pink but I can't, it makes me look positively sallow! And now I'm getting jealous—when I was your age I would not have been allowed to dress in anything as flirty as a sun-dress. How times change for the better!'

Zoe accepted her mother-in-law's assessment of her appearance with a questioning smile. Did a deliberately artlessly piled top knot and a strappy sun-dress that moulded the upper part of her body and flared from her hips to a short skirt constitute flirty? And did Javier think so? The brevity of the tight smile he lobbed in her general direction as he arranged toasted rolls on a linen napkin gave her the distinct impression the jury was out on that one.

'Come.' Isabella Maria took Zoe's hand. 'Let us wait outside and leave my menfolk to the chores they say I am incapable of managing. I've heard it said,' she confided as they emerged onto the terrace and the sunlit mid-morning, 'that the kitchen is the heart of the home, or the engine room—take your pick. Me, I prefer to know nothing about it.'

Settling her narrow skirt, she sat at the table in the shade of an angled parasol. 'My son informs me that he dispensed with Teresa's excellent services because you and he wished to be alone. Does that mean there is something wrong? Tell me—' dark eyes took on a gimlet quality, at variance with her smiling mouth '—do you make my son happy? Do sit—' she gestured to the chair nearest hers '—and tell me.'

Zoe inhaled a deep breath of jasmine-scented warm air, not prepared to even hazard a guess as to the answer to that question. Taking her seat, she folded her hands demurely in her lap and asked one back, 'On the day of my wedding you said you were glad Javier had taken your advice and married me; do you remember?'

She hadn't given the remark much thought at the time, but now she was beginning to wonder if there had been more to his proposal than the desire of an honourable man to keep her out of the vicinity of gold-diggers of the male persuasion until she was more mature and able to make the right decisions.

The older woman's tinkling laugh sliced through the drowsy silence of the morning like a cleaver. 'Of course I remember. How could I forget that that son of mine actually took my advice for the first time in his stubborn life? I suppose he thought about what I'd said—though he took his time about it—and realised that it made perfect sense.'

An icy fist closed around Zoe's heart and her voice sounded tinny to her own ears as she asked, 'What did you say to him?'

'The obvious—that he should marry you because you're a considerable heiress!'

Again the high-pitched tinkling laugh that set Zoe's teeth on edge and produced the beginnings of what promised to be a pounding headache.

Isabella Maria's voice lowered confidentially. 'Since my son turned eighteen he's been targeted by the type of woman whose only asset is her looks. He's a handsome brute with much charisma and, above all, wealth. Natural prey for a woman on the hunt.'

She sketched a tiny shrug. 'Like any mother, I'll admit to wanting to see him settled and happy and producing my grandchildren. But I dreaded the thought that he might fall into the clutches of some dreadful creature whose main interest in him was the size of his bank balance. Apart from the common sense of the tradition of wealth marrying wealth, with money of your own I knew that if he asked you to be his wife, and you accepted, it would be because you truly loved him for himself.'

'I've always loved him!' Zoe found herself blurting, the admission wrung from her as if she had no control over her own tongue.

'And he adores you,' the older woman announced complacently. 'I saw that on the day of your wedding.'

Zoe lowered her eyes. She could feel her mouth

begin to tremble. Her mother-in-law knew nothing; she saw what she wanted to see. The only things Javier had felt for her on their wedding day had been a mild affection, a sort of habit thing that had started years ago when he'd taken pity on an orphaned kid, and a teeth-gritting exasperation because in his opinion the grown-up kid had been in danger of going off the rails.

And as for marrying her because she had money of her own, well—dream on! The funds held in trust for her might seem large to most people, but Javier would regard them as little more than pocket money.

And when Isabella Maria said archly, 'Now all I have to do is wait for my first grandchild,' Zoe had a hard time stopping herself from bursting into tears because a child with her was something Javier was desperate not to have. She'd seen the grin of relief on his too-handsome face when she'd broken what he'd obviously regarded as the welcome news to him, hadn't she?

Thankfully the unwanted tête-à-tête was broken when the menfolk appeared with loaded trays. But hardly had the contents been set out on the table than Javier said grimly, 'You'll have to excuse me, I have to make a phone call,' and strode back inside the villa.

To get in touch with Glenda, set her mind at rest? Tell her he was missing her, too. That he was only here in Spain with the wife who was nothing more than a self-inflicted burden because she'd gone off her trolley, threatening to walk out on him before he, in his so-superior wisdom, deemed she was fit to look after herself. And would he dare to confess that he'd been unfaithful to his mistress and had sex with his wife?

Cutting off that manic train of thought before it led her into the murky realms of the completely ridiculous, she tuned into the argument that was going on between her in-laws.

'But we've only just got here! Am I not allowed to spend time with my own son? I refuse to believe that Javier—'

'Izzy,' Lionel cut in firmly with an apologetic look in Zoe's direction. 'Don't be difficult. We have the day here and this evening we leave for Almeria. The hotel room is booked. I've already told you how Javier explained that, as he had no time to give Zoe the honeymoon she deserved straight after the wedding ceremony—'

With a pallid smile and a murmur of excuse, Zoe left the table, her breakfast untouched. Her stomach was churning and her legs felt like cotton wool and only carried her as far as the carved stone balustrade. She leant there, grateful for the support, her eyes fixed unseeingly on the wide expanse of manicured lawn, the romantically wild garden beyond and far below the cove where the blue sea creamed gently against the soft white sand.

She knew how fond Javier was of both his parents. Normally he would have welcomed them with open arms. But nothing about this so-called honeymoon in such a perfect venue was normal.

While Isabella Maria had been talking to her out here Javier must have put a romantic spin on his need to be alone with his wife. Why? Because the future of their marriage was approaching crunch time and he wouldn't want anyone around when he told her he now agreed with her earlier statement that they should call it a day?

Or was he aiming to make this a real honeymoon? After they'd come so close to making love again this morning she could almost believe it. But Glenda's obvious involvement in his life, the length of time he was spending on the phone to her, rather knocked that belief on the head.

Giving a muffled groan, Zoe silently admitted that she didn't know whether she was on her head or her heels. The only constant was her addiction to him, the intense craving for his love, the one thing she needed to make her life complete, the one thing she didn't look like getting.

'How many times have I told you not to stay out in the sun without a hat?'

At the sound of his voice her stomach twisted into sick knots. A hand on her burning shoulder turned her. Her eyes locked with his. He was more gorgeous than any man had a right to be; he would turn female heads wherever he went, break female hearts—

'Get back under the shade. Have you eaten a proper breakfast?'

Once again he was treating her like a large, not-too-bright child. But the grim look was gone. Those smoky eyes were smiling. His conversation with Glenda must have been successful. In the reassurance department?

Frustratedly admitting that now wasn't the time to touch on the subject of his mistress past—and pres-

ent?—Zoe listened to his gently apologetic words as
he escorted her back to the table beneath the shade
of the parasol. 'As I've virtually shown my folks the
door, we're going to have to make them feel really
welcome for the rest of the day.' Leaving her to pon-
der that his uncharacteristic behaviour in telling his
beloved parents to scarper must have stemmed from
something really important.

Giving his unwanted wife her marching orders?

Or making wild passionate love to her, non-stop,
no time for noticing anyone else existed?

Of the two possible scenarios she knew which one
she was fervently praying for.

Ten minutes after returning to the villa, replete with
a late lunch—the quayside lobster had lived up to its
reputation—they were all relaxing on the terrace at
Javier's insistence when the whup-whup of rotor
blades broke through the sleepy silence.

Isabella Maria gave a prolonged screech when the
craft landed on the lawn below the terrace. 'Are we
being invaded!'

'Relax, Mama.' Javier grinned, rising to his feet.
'Look at the logo. It's one of ours, not the mafia!'

One of the construction company's fleet, Zoe recognised from the world-famous logo, curiosity momentarily ousting the inner tension that had been eating at her since this morning.

A dapper little guy with slicked-back black hair,
wearing an immaculate pinstriped suit, emerged from
his seat beside the pilot carrying a leather briefcase.
Must-do work for Javier's eyes only? Zoe pondered

as he mounted the steps to the terrace, noting the man's obsequious bow in Javier's direction as he laid the case reverentially on the table.

'Señor Garcia,' Javier introduced, mentioning a renowned Madrid jeweller, taking the proffered key and unlocking the case himself, opening it to display a glittering array of rings on midnight-blue velvet.

'Fabuloso!' Isabella Maria squealed, her dark eyes winging from her son's to the jewels and back again. *'Por qué? Quién?'*

Ignoring her, Javier turned the force of his bone-melting smile on Zoe. 'You never did have an engagement ring. This morning I decided to arrange to correct that omission.'

Her breath went as her heart danced beneath her breasts, her eyes blurring until the display of costly rings became a kaleidoscope of colour and glittering lights. And when Javier came to stand behind her, laying a light hand on her naked shoulder, she quivered, the exquisite sensation of his skin against her skin leaving her feeling light-headed and as weak as a newborn kitten.

'They are all your ring size—choose whichever you like best,' he murmured as Señor Garcia moved discreetly away.

Lionel announced, 'Time to go, Izzy. And don't put that look on your face!'

In the flurry of goodbyes—reluctant on Isabella Maria's part, with her pressing invitations to visit with them at their summer home—Zoe was being thoroughly cross with herself for thinking bad things about her gorgeous husband. He hadn't been glued to the phone for ages murmuring sweet nothings into his ex-mistress's ear—he'd been arranging transport for Garcia and his wildly expensive collection of gems.

Just for her!

He wouldn't have made such an impulsive gesture if he wanted rid of her!

She didn't deserve him she decided, going all misty-eyed, turning to gaze up at him when they were finally alone again. 'You can be really romantic,' she breathed, her heart swelling with love, wondering if he could read it in her eyes.

But he simply gave her that sizzling smile and a laconic, '"Romantic" turns you on?' wondering why he hadn't taken that tack much earlier on instead of all that Mr Nice Guy stuff.

'You turn me on,' Zoe confessed honestly, as just looking at him, tall, dark, spectacularly lean and powerful, sent rivers of sexual anticipation scalding through her bloodstream.

'So I have noticed,' Javier slotted in with massive male satisfaction, graphically reminding her of the way she had wholeheartedly and very actively encouraged his earlier and never-to-be-forgotten sexual attentions.

Deciding to ignore that rather humiliating observation, she did what his hand gesture commanded and concentrated on the selection of rings.

Impossible to make a choice, they were all so beautiful. Unused to seeing his Zoe in a state of dither, Javier selected an enormous yellow diamond in a sleekly modern gold setting and slid it onto her finger to sit beside her plain gold wedding band.

'It's too big!' Sunlight caught the facets of the costly stone as Javier held her hand out to assess the way it looked against her long, slender fingers.

'Unmissable,' he confirmed. 'Don't you like it?'

'Love it,' she admitted around the sudden lump in her throat. 'But it's got to be wickedly expensive.'

'So?' Javier gave the uninterested shrug of a man to whom money was no object. Then lifted her hand to his lips and slowly kissed the tips of her fingers, noting the rosy flush that spread across her delicate cheekbones, the rapid pulse beat at the base of her long, elegant throat, the peaking of her exquisite breasts beneath the fine fabric that covered them so lovingly; and congratulated himself on getting the hang of 'romantic'.

Contemplating his next move—after he'd got rid of Garcia and the chopper—involving bed and the extraction of promises never again to even think about walking away from their marriage, he bit back a violent oath when his mobile interrupted his imagery of how he would undress her with much lingering at strategic areas.

His bitten acknowledgement of who was speaking was followed by an immediate descent of arching black brows as he handed the instrument to Zoe. 'Your grandmother's companion.'

Puzzled, Zoe took it. She'd had no contact with Grandmother Alice since her wedding day except for an unchatty card at Christmas time.

The usually taciturn older woman was alarmingly garrulous, not allowing Zoe to get a word in edgewise. 'I'm not supposed to be telling you this but your grandmother's failing fast. Nothing specific. Just old age and a feeble heart. I know she wants to make her peace with you before anything happens. She's fretting and it isn't good for her. She's got the idea into her head that she didn't treat you as well as she should have done. I did suggest that I might ask you to visit with her but she all but bit my head off. She's adamant that if you wanted to see her you'd come without being asked. Very stubborn, your grandmother. So, if you do come, don't tell her I contacted you. She'd be furious with me and that wouldn't do at all, not in her state of health. It might finish her off.'

Watching the colour leach out of Zoe's face, Javier reached for the phone, gave his name and listened to a repeat of the sorry tale. Eventually he spoke. 'Zoe will be with you as soon as is humanly possible.' And cut the connection, the strong slant of his cheekbones taut as he turned to her, wanting to take fate by the throat and throttle it for stepping in and ruining his plans for the wooing of his wife, pushing him in a direction he didn't want to travel.

Forcing a deep breath into his lungs, he made himself relax, stop beefing. An old lady was fading; what right had he to get in a selfish strop about it?

He had never approved of the way Alice Rothwell had treated her orphaned granddaughter but if she was regretting it now, then she deserved to know that at the end she was forgiven. And it would help Zoe, too. That was the most important thing, knowing that the cold, outwardly unloving woman did have some affection for her.

His voice cool, carefully unrevealing of his feelings, he resigned his definitely hopeful-looking plan of seducing his wife until she was inredeemably hooked on him to the back burner and said, 'We'd best get a move on,' and punched in the numbers required to put the company jet on standby.

CHAPTER NINE

IT WAS dark when the sleek company car finally drew up outside her grandmother's house. With a feeling of foreboding Zoe glanced at the neat façade, the scene of so much childhood unhappiness. But if the stern, unloving old lady wanted to clear her conscience then she was prepared to do all she could to facilitate it.

With a terse instruction to the driver to wait, Javier handed Zoe out and extracted her small, hastily packed suitcase from the boot. Two firm strides brought him back to her, and strong yet gentle hands were positioned on either side of her face, tilting her head so that he could look directly into her eyes by the light from the street lamp. 'Sweetheart, would you like me to stay here with you? I've a feeling this won't be easy.'

Zoe would like nothing better but she smothered the desire to say yes, please. She couldn't be that selfish. There would be no point in him kicking his heels in this gloomy house with two dour old ladies whose idea of a fun evening was criticising the neighbours.

'No. Honestly, I'll be fine.' She loved the touch of his hands against her skin, adored the way the lamp light threw his strong bone structure into such stunning relief, felt so strengthened and warmed by his kindness. The inherent kindness she'd instinctively picked up on as a child and had benefited from— admittedly with one or two blips, which had been all her own fault—throughout her time of knowing him.

'I guess this—whatever this is—is something Grandmother Alice and I have to deal with ourselves. You'd only feel like a spare part.'

Javier's thoughts exactly. Little as he wanted to be separated from her, not even for a night, when things seemed to be going in the direction he wanted them to go, he knew that she and Alice Rothwell needed the space to at least reach some kind of understanding.

'I'll only stay a week.' Zoe's voice sounded very small as she contemplated that length of separation. But if Grandmother Alice was coming to the end of her life she deserved the relief of getting what she apparently now saw as past wrongs off her chest, to find absolution. After all, the old lady hadn't wanted the responsibility of bringing her up after the untimely and tragic death of her own son and his wife. But she had taken her in when she might have had her put in a children's home.

Javier gritted his teeth and swallowed his stinging objection to what seemed more like a life sentence than a week out of his life. Curving his fingers around her delicate cheekbones, he lowered his head and, unable to stop it happening, captured her lips with raw passion.

Instinctively, desperately, Zoe kissed him back, fiery desire flooding through every inch of her body as she strained against him, tiny tremors racing through her veins as she clung, fingers lacing into the soft silkiness of his hair, lifting her hips provocatively against the all-male hardness of his. A low moan broke from her throat and then, without warning, he dropped his hands and stepped away from her.

'I'll see you safely inside,' he virtually grated at her, avoiding the shocked widening of her fantastic golden eyes, just about loathing himself for having started something he couldn't finish.

Lifting the suitcase he'd abandoned on the pavement in one hand, Javier placed the other firmly on the small of her back, urging her into the driveway. His body felt as if it were on fire, burning for her, aching for her. One more second and he knew he'd have lost all hope of control, stripped her beautiful body naked on the pavement and made passionate love to her in full view of his driver and any passerby. No other woman had ever brought him to the teetering brink of losing all control, but, oh, the things his Zoe did to him…!

Glancing up at his tense profile, Zoe felt cold and abandoned, shivering as the sensation of nausea claimed her stomach. Why had he kissed her like that then pushed her away as if he disgusted himself?

Or was her immediate and over-the-top eagerness in the response department what had disgusted him? Did he prefer his women to be more laid-back and coolly sophisticated where his sexual advances were concerned?

His women! The image of Glenda Havers' sultry face pinged into her mind. Was she, Zoe, just another female for him to slake his lust on? Was that all she meant to him? Was she already beginning to bore him?

He'd certainly pulled out all the stops when it had come to grasping the excuse to get her out of his hair when they'd received the news of Grandmother Alice's frail and fading condition. Hitching a ride in the helicopter, transferring to the company jet in Madrid, the car waiting at the airport to ferry them here—

Oh, put a sock in it!

Zoe gave herself a furious mental kick for her dreadful habit of putting the worst possible interpretation on everything he did. In getting her back to England before she could catch her breath he'd only been doing what he automatically did best—clicking his fingers and making things happen.

And he'd had that fabulous selection of rings flown in for her, hadn't he? How could she possibly forget that? Sometimes she really despised herself!

Another savage mental kick had her deciding she was behaving like a mixed-up brat. Apart from her lost parents, no one had ever loved her, so she'd assumed no one ever would.

Oliver had said he loved her, but she was clued-up enough to know that the only thing he loved was the thought of her future inheritance.

And as for Javier—well, even employing positive thinking she just didn't know! Not beyond a shadow of a doubt. Did he want their marriage to last beyond the two years he'd stipulated, or didn't he?

Her voice driven, she impressed, 'Javier, we really do have to have that talk.'

'Of course.' Icy cool. He pressed his finger to the doorbell, his naturally powerful, dominant personality leading him to point out with impersonal factuality, 'But not here, not now.'

His gut clenched as he recalled the plans he'd made for this night. He wasn't ready to lay his heart on the line for her in case it got trampled on, but he sure as hell had aimed to romance her, seduce her, make endless love to her until she became as addicted to him as he was to her and would forget her former intention to walk out of their marriage. Plans that would have to wait for another week before they could be put into the action he craved.

Dire frustration made his voice curter than was polite when the door swung slowly open to reveal Miss Pilkington—if the housekeeper/companion had a Christian name he had never heard it—who said with horror, 'You can't come in at this time of night. She'll know it's not a normal visit.'

'This isn't the time for that kind of game,' he countered immediately. 'If Alice is fretting as much as you say she is, she'll forget to be annoyed with you when she knows how quickly Zoe responded to your message.'

Urging her over the threshold, impatience etched on every line of his darkly handsome features, he clipped out, 'I'll be at the London apartment, Zoe. Call me if you need anything at all.'

The hand that lifted to caress the side of her lovely face, touch her soft, warm, silky skin, was quickly stuffed back in the pocket of his well-cut chinos. Touching her at all in the state he was in would be a bad mistake. His plans were shelved, end of story. Accept it. Why pile on more torment?

With a brusque nod in no particular direction he swung on his heel before he found himself making an utter prat of himself and punching holes in the wall, leaving Zoe to watch his departure with bleak eyes, wondering if she would ever understand him.

'Now are you sure you're all right, Grandmother?' Zoe had armed the old lady out into the sunlit garden and now settled the light woollen rug around her knees. Even under the circumstances of the new rapprochement the use of Granny, or, worse still, Gran would have brought a forbidding frown to those stern features.

'Perfectly.' Momentarily, those features softened as a gnarled old hand reached out to pat Zoe's, and then, typically, she spoiled the moment by opining, 'You've turned out to have a cool head on your shoulders. Your upbringing—which you know I've been feeling slightly uncomfortable about—didn't do any damage, quite the contrary.'

Zoe bit back the response that any improvement had been brought about by Javier's taking over the responsibility for her when she'd been sixteen years old and as bolshie as they came.

Let the old lady keep her illusions if they helped her! And the cool head she'd mentioned was a reference to the way her granddaughter had taken over, vetting and hiring a new housekeeper, an energetic widow in her fifties who wanted something to occupy her and was more than happy to live in, enabling her to sell the marital home and invest the proceeds for her retirement.

That had left the ageing and grudgingly grateful Miss Pilkington to concentrate on the companion side of her duties, and against her grandmother's wishes she'd called in her GP, who had given the old lady a lecture about not consulting him earlier and prescribed essential medication, which already seemed to be working well.

All achieved in five hectic days. Her duty done, Zoe felt free to leave, free to go to Javier earlier than either of them had expected.

Excitement bubbled up inside her. She couldn't wait!

They would have that delayed discussion about the future of their relationship. The suspense of not knowing had been giving her sleepless nights, tying her brain in knots.

Slim fingers automatically touched the yellow diamond ring that had become a talisman of hope. She flashed a smile as her grandmother's companion came out to sit with her charge.

'I'll make tracks now,' she stated, trying not to look too insultingly over the moon at the prospect. She dropped a light kiss on her grandmother's papery cheek. 'I'll keep in touch. Take care and don't chicken out of your appointment next week for that thorough hospital check-up.'

She felt so light-hearted she practically skipped over the smoothly manicured lawn to the house where her already-packed suitcase was waiting in the hall.

Javier had proposed an empty marriage out of a

wearisome sense of duty and had shown his complete lack of interest in it by his increasingly regular absences. But something had changed on the night they'd spent making frantic and utterly wonderful love to each other. Something really basic.

He didn't love her, not yet anyway; she knew that and had to be sensible and accept it. But even though it probably went against the grain with him, he did desire her. He wasn't able to hide that. Couple that with his long-standing though sometimes sorely tried affection for her, add in her devoted love for him, and they could make a good, lasting marriage. He might even, given time, change his mind and want her to have his child.

Her car was waiting for her on the driveway. Javier had had it delivered to her the day after he'd deposited her here. The note on the dashboard had stated, 'I thought you might like to snatch half an hour of freedom now and then—drive carefully!'

His thoughtfulness had warmed her heart to a rosy glow and that evening when she'd phoned the apartment to thank him no one had been home. He hadn't been picking up his mobile, either, so she'd left a message, and in the hustle to get everything arranged here she hadn't tried to contact him again.

Stowing her suitcase on the back seat, she smiled wryly. Trust him to land her back with the granny-going-shopping job instead of the mightily disapproved-of Lotus sports! No matter, she was on her way back to him! She'd make the journey in a milk float, if she had to.

*   *   *

Her smile for the janitor was still wreathing her face as Zoe used the security card that activated the lift to the London apartment. It was late afternoon and knowing Javier he wouldn't be sitting home reading a good book. He'd be dishing out orders at Head Office, getting his head down to some hard graft.

Dismissing the very real temptation to call him at his office to let him know she was here and waiting, she decided to surprise him. A long hot bath, lots of care with her make-up before she slipped into something slinky and revealing to remind him that he did find her sexually desirable.

Her cheeks reddening at the thought of setting out to seduce her own husband, she let herself into the spacious apartment and stumbled into a massive cream leather suitcase, the resulting thump bringing forth a trilling, 'Javier, darling, is that you?'

Every last vestige of colour leached from Zoe's face as a nauseating knot cramped in her stomach. She would know that drawly voice anywhere and her worst nightmare was confirmed when Glenda Havers emerged into the vast sitting room clad in a short black silk robe that clung to her voluptuous curves.

Zoe's heart seemed to be beating at the base of her throat. She couldn't speak for the clenching pain of jealousy and the far deeper one of betrayal. It was Glenda who broke the short stinging silence.

'Oh, dear!' She raised her baby-blue eyes to the ceiling and sketched a tiny shrug. 'We didn't expect you for another couple of days.'

Ignoring that painfully obvious statement, Zoe swallowed convulsively and found the scratchy remnants of her voice. She knew what was going on but she had to ask, 'What are you doing here?'

'Oh, come on!' The cherry-red lips curved in a small pitying smile as the other woman wandered further into the room on clouds of musky perfume. 'What do you think?' Pushing a languid hand through her tousled mane of rich brown hair, Glenda sank onto a sofa, tucking her legs beneath her, utterly relaxed, quite at home, Zoe thought on a stab of bitterness.

'Listen, kid, wise up.' Narrowed blue eyes flicked away from Zoe to minutely scrutinise her fingernails, as if she was searching for flaws in the cherry-red varnish. 'You're due to come into a pretty hefty chunk of the folding stuff—why else did you think Javier married you? The last time I teased him about cradle-snatching—when we were in Cannes, I think it was—he admitted it. Not that his marriage came between us, of course. We've been lovers for years, as you knew. But you weren't supposed to know it was still definitely ongoing; we have been very discreet. But now it's out in the open, you'll have to decide what to do about it.'

The inspection of her nails completed, she raised narrowed, heavily lashed eyes to Zoe's white face. 'Face the fact that Javier would have turned on the charm to keep you unsuspecting and doting—a wealthy wife is better than a poor one, and all that,' she derided. 'But my advice, for what it's worth, is cut loose before the sexy bastard breaks your girly little heart.'

'What time is he expected?' Zoe pushed out between clenched teeth, bitter anger taking over. What she'd first believed was an insane nightmare, something she'd crazily hoped could be explained away, was now cold, hard fact. If he walked in now she would kill him!

Just for a moment the luscious brunette seemed disconcerted but Zoe decided she had to have been imagining it when Glenda managed a tiny shrug and drawled, 'No idea. Some time tonight. Something needing his urgent attention cropped up in Milan. We decided it wasn't worth my going with him, as usual, so I'm to wait here. So do try to be adult about the situation and either learn to accept it, or, far better from your point of view, cut free.'

Accept it! Never in this life!

Pain throbbed in her temples and sizzling rage tied her insides in crippling knots.

Accepting the sordid situation wasn't an option. And neither was staying to confront him. She'd only end up giving herself away, allowing him to see how thoroughly he'd broken her heart. She wouldn't give the louse the satisfaction!

Which left the other. Zoe turned on her heel and walked out.

CHAPTER TEN

How she'd ever got back to Wakeham Lodge without ending up as an RTA statistic, Zoe would never know. She remembered absolutely nothing of the drive out of London, her tortured mind being completely occupied with the pain and humiliation of what Glenda had made her face.

But she made it in one piece in time to walk into the large homely kitchen just as Ethel was heating the milk for the early bedtime cocoa.

'Are you all right?' It was Joe who noticed her silent appearance first, rising from the long scrubbed pine table, a look of concern on his weathered face.

So she must look as awful as she felt, Zoe reflected heavily. Sketching what she hoped would pass for a reassuring smile, she offered, 'I'm fine.'

If you could call feeling dead inside and brutally mangled at one and the same time fine, that was.

Ethel swung round from the vast Aga cooker, taking the pan off the heat. 'We didn't expect you—you should have phoned to let us know you were coming. Another half an hour and Joe would have bolted the doors for the night! Is Javier here with you?'

'No.' Zoe pulled out a chair from the table and sat down before her wobbly legs gave way beneath her. Javier would be back in London by now, sure to be. With his mistress. Sick as a parrot because he'd been found out? Or would he merely shrug those magnificent shoulders of his and write off his losses?

Isabella Maria had openly rejoiced that her son had taken her advice for the first time in his life. Wealth should marry wealth. How she'd scorned that concept back at the villa, ruled it out of play, believing she knew him better than his mother did! She now knew it to be hatefully true.

Two mugs of cocoa appeared on the table. 'Let me get you something—a little light supper. How about scrambled eggs and bacon? At least a nice cup of tea and a slice of hot buttered toast?' Ethel laid a light hand on her shoulder. 'You look a bit peaky.'

There was a natural curiosity there as well as concern, Zoe recognised. She tried out a smile. Her mouth felt unnaturally stiff. 'Thanks, but I've already eaten.'

Not a lie, not exactly. She'd eaten breakfast this morning. It seemed a million light years away. How could a day start with such bright hope and end a few hours later in black misery and complete disillusionment?

'I've been spending a few days with Grandmother Alice while—Javier's—' her tongue almost refused to form his name '—while he's been away on business.'

This time without his precious mistress. Oh, how she hated him!

At the sound of her voice Boysie stirred in his basket at the side of the Aga. One eye opened, his tail gave just one half-hearted thump of recognition before he went right back to sleep again.

Nothing like the usual ecstatic welcome. Her eyes flooded with weak tears, she blinked them back furiously as a lump the size of a house brick lodged in her throat. She felt rejected, a waste of space.

As if tuned in to her feelings, or maybe because he'd noticed her brimming eyes, Joe explained kindly, 'The little fella's bushed. I practically walked the legs off him this evening.'

'And spent most of the afternoon throwing his ball for him. Honestly, he's like an overgrown kid with that little dog,' Ethel put in fondly.

Zoe had to be glad that Boysie wasn't pining for her. That was the sensible and adult way of looking at the situation. But right now she felt as she had done when she'd first gone to live with her grandmother. As if she was of no importance to anyone, as if the loss she'd suffered was too great to be borne.

'I think I'll turn in now, it's been a long day.' A truly dreadful day. A stab at a yawn to indicate tiredness before she said her goodnights. She knew she wouldn't sleep a wink.

Seeking her old room, she collected a glass of Javier's whisky on the way in the hope that it would knock her out, stop her thinking.

It didn't. Tormented emotions kept her staring into the darkness. She'd had a few easily dismissed suspicions in the past, but why hadn't she guessed that the mistress who had lasted far longer than most in his bachelor life was still firmly in it?

She must have been laughably naive to believe for one moment that a man so highly sexed and sophisticated would have been content to remain celibate during the first barren year of their marriage.

Instead of her silly schoolgirlish fantasies of teaching him to fall head over heels in love with her, she should have faced the uncomfortable fact that Javier would want a real woman—a woman with Glenda's obvious sexual experience, sultry mouth and voluptuous body—not a green and gangly girl, which she was sure was the way he continued to see her.

In the small hours it came to her that even the last, incredibly slender hope that—overlooking the plain fact that Glenda had been installed in the London apartment—for some warped reason of her own the other woman had been lying through her teeth, was dead in the water.

He'd been expected back from Milan this evening. Hours ago. Glenda had, as he'd instructed, been eagerly waiting for him.

Cat got the cream.

Would the other woman have broken the news that his wife had walked in and discovered her? Of course she would, if only to have warned him.

If Javier had been innocent and he'd arranged for Glenda to meet him at the apartment for some reason or other he would have completed his business with her, got rid of her and phoned her, Zoe, to let her know he was back at the apartment.

Ditching that unlikely scenario, she impressed the other on her overtired mind. Javier guilty, guilty as hell. The luscious Glenda greeting her lover with the news that their ongoing affair had been uncovered. His child bride taking off at speed.

If he'd had any respect for her at all, cared a toss for her well-being, he would have done everything he could to contact her. Not to beg her to go back to him—even he with his massive ego would see that that was impossible—but to make sure she was all right.

In the darkness she dragged the magnificent diamond ring off her finger and hurled it with force into a corner. A bauble to keep her sweet. As Glenda had maliciously pointed out, he'd turn on the charm to keep her unsuspecting and doting.

And he hadn't attempted to touch her, much less make love to her until that night when she'd told him she'd had enough, that as far as she was concerned their paper marriage was over, she reminded herself furiously. He'd seen his callous plan to keep his father's one-time partner's fortune wedded to his own fly out of the window. So he'd gritted his teeth, done his duty.

Her wide gold wedding band followed the diamond.

Ethel watched Zoe's descent of the main staircase with anxious eyes. She looked different. Older and harder. Her long blonde hair was piled in an elegant knot on top of her head, her slim body clad in deep turquoise silk that positively shrieked designer chic.

As usual since she'd arrived here out of the blue, alone, her ring finger was bare. Something was wrong with that marriage, very wrong. The past three days she'd been as jumpy as a kitten on a bed of hot coals, leaping out of her skin every time the phone rang, never leaving the grounds, pacing, always pacing, her straining eyes turned in the direction of the long drive.

This evening there was a marked difference. A difference that left Ethel feeling even more anxious.

'Don't wait up, Ethel,' Zoe said as soon as her high-heeled mules hit the floor of the hall. 'I'll take the main door key so ask Joe not to bolt it when he locks up for the night.'

Ethel was well aware that Javier's name hadn't crossed his wife's lips since she'd arrived late on Monday evening. Nevertheless, in case her employer did phone and ask to speak to his wife, she felt it incumbent to ask, 'Where are you going?'

For long moments Ethel didn't think she was going to get an answer. Zoe turned slowly on her heel, her suddenly and newly imperious eyes conveying the message that a child she was not, and would not be treated like one. Her titular status as mistress of the house had never been more strikingly in evidence.

'To look in on Jenny and Guy's housewarming party. The invitation was in the post waiting for my attention.' A tiny pause when something of the old impetuous, heartbreakingly needy Zoe looked out from those clear golden eyes, then a frigidly cool, 'Good night, Ethel.'

The early evening sun warmed Zoe's skin but didn't reach the cold spot inside her as she stood on the drive, stowing the main door key in her purse and searching for her car keys.

It was over. Three whole days of waiting for Javier to try to track her down if only to discuss the ending of their marriage, never mind one human being's natural concern for another.

He didn't give a damn!

Three endless days and nights of wanting to see him face to face one last time, for the release of telling him exactly what she thought of him, calling him all the bad names she could think of, getting the pain and the poison out of her system.

It wasn't going to happen.

So she had taken a long, hard look at the pathetic creature she had become and taken the decision to put it all behind her. Get on with her life. Forget he'd ever been in it.

As she drove to Jenny's brand-new home, part of an exclusive development on the outskirts of the village, she mentally ticked off her plans for the future.

Start divorce proceedings. Contact her trustees to ask for a release of sufficient funds to buy a small flat close to her place of voluntary work. Take up the Chair's suggestion that she make herself responsible for parting the wealthy from some of their excess funds.

And then—The 'And then' bit presented itself as a black hole, a yawning, featureless empty space. Zoe firmed her lush mouth and floored the accelerator.

'Sweetie, I'm so glad you could come.' Jenny tucked her arm through Zoe's as she proudly showed her over her new home. 'I sent the invitation on the off-chance. No one seemed to know where you and Javier were. Why isn't he with you?' She rolled her eyes.

'That husband of yours would have added a touch of class!'

'Working.' Zoe wasn't prepared to discuss the ending of her marriage, and she didn't want to talk about him, or even think about him ever again. 'I love those curtains,' she changed the subject rapidly.

'Great, aren't they? Look.' Easily diverted, Jenny picked up a remote and the heavy linen drapes swished back and forth. Zoe smiled her dutiful smile until her face ached and quashed the wish that she had never come. She had to learn to make a life of her own. And mixing with the old gang was a beginning.

'Now you must see the kitchen. It's got every gadget under the sun. Guy went bananas when he saw the size of the bill. Now all I have to do is learn to cook!'

Five minutes later, a glass of white wine in her hands, Zoe joined the other guests outside on the patio where most of the menfolk were gathered around the barbecue, drinking beer from cans, the laughter level rising, multicoloured fairy lights twinkling on the trellis as evening shadows lengthened over the garden, the smell of cooking meat turning her stomach.

Oliver Sherman was chatting up a redhead in a very small black dress. Zoe turned her back on him, joining a group of female acquaintances. Oliver was not one of the old gang she wanted to mix with!

But seconds later a voice at her shoulder told her he had other ideas. 'Welcome back to the fold. Looking for some fun without that grim husband of yours?'

Zoe swallowed a sigh. Here we go again! she agitated, remembering the horrible scene at Guy and Jenny's wedding reception and the shattering aftermath. She turned slightly, half facing him, and drawled coolly, 'Oliver, don't be such a bore.'

And then her face flamed with immediate colour, her flesh burning on her bones because Javier had emerged onto the patio with Glenda firmly in tow.

How dared he? How could he? If he wanted to humiliate her, demonstrate that his mistress took precedence in his life, he couldn't have chosen a better method! She wanted to fall into a hole in the ground and never, ever, be seen again!

Blood thundering in her ears, she felt the heightened colour wash out of her face, leaving her ashen and cold. So cold she was shaking.

As usual he looked spectacular: tall, lean, urbane, dressed in beautifully cut pale grey chinos and a black shirt that somehow made the impressive breadth of his shoulders even more intimidating. And the impact of his darkly handsome face, all arrogant angles and brooding smoky eyes, stunned her into the drainingly painful recognition of all she had lost.

She couldn't lose what she had never had was her immediate self-protective counter-thought, and that smack-in-the-eye fact had her entertaining the wild idea of getting up close and intimate with the still-hovering Sherman just to pay her adulterous husband back.

An idea just as swiftly jettisoned. She would hate herself for ever if she stooped that low.

As his eyes found her amongst the guests Zoe knew

she couldn't feel any lower than she did right at this moment, whatever she did.

Even with his mistress glued to his side she only had to see him to be swept by a wave of longing that was frightening in its intensity. How low, how stupid could a girl get?

As he strode towards where she was standing her stomach tied itself in painful knots, her heart started racing as people automatically made way for him, deferring to his dominant personality, female eyes widening with admiration, male glances a mixture of awe and envy.

Helplessly, her own eyes were riveted on that devastatingly lean and handsome face. Was she the only person who came into contact with him able to hold her own? And, far more importantly, could she hold her own now, in this humiliating situation? Or would her battered and bleeding heart betray her?

His features were hard and unyielding as he reached her but there was one of his charismatic smiles for their hostess as she hustled up with a tray of drinks. 'You have a lovely home, Jenny. I hope you and Guy will be truly happy here. But now, I'm afraid I'm going to have to drag my wife away.'

Taking Zoe's untouched glass from her suddenly limp and unresisting fingers, he placed it on the tray. Smoke-grey eyes held hers with stark intent. 'Shall we?'

A rhetorical question, Zoe recognised, panic setting in because quite obviously he and Glenda were going to present a united front when he admitted they were still lovers, and spelled out that, now it was out in the open, there was no point in continuing to stay in this misbegotten marriage, not even for a further year.

As his guiding hand cupped her elbow Zoe wanted to leap up, fasten her own hands around his throat and strangle him. For taking the initiative—she had wanted to be the one to confront him, demand a divorce with her new-found icy cool, sweep out leaving him looking and feeling small! For his effortless ability to steal her heart—and keep it—damn him!

Tears weren't far away as they reached the pavement outside the house. His car was parked on the other side of the smart new cul-de-sac. Was he intending to say his piece here then whisk his gloating mistress away, leaving her standing alone, humiliated and hurting?

Zoe's small chin came up, her spine stiffening, bracing herself for what was to come, and for the first time she let her eyes rest on Glenda for longer than the split second it had initially taken her to register the other woman's presence beside Javier.

It was almost dusk now but still easy to see that the other woman's smooth confidence had deserted her. Her shoulders slumped and her mouth drooped. Was her conscience pricking? Was that what was making her look so miserable? Whatever, Zoe didn't want her pity.

Dragging her arm from Javier's restraining hand, Zoe reminded herself of how very much she should violently hate him and lashed out through clenched teeth, 'I don't know what the two of you think you're going to achieve by muscling in on my evening with friends.'

'You will,' he came back grimly, his hand capturing her wrist now in a vice-like grip. 'Tell her, Glenda. Or I stop that cheque.'

'I…I…' Baby-blue eyes were fastened on the pavement. She pulled in a shaky huff of breath and muttered, 'I lied.'

'And—?' Javier prompted with a bite.

Glenda's cheeks turned a dull red as she turned a look of loathing on Zoe. 'Javier and I were finished well before he married you,' she pushed out quickly, her voice low and sulky.

Zoe's heart jumped like a landed fish. She wanted to believe what she was hearing but didn't dare to. The other woman was putting on a convincing performance. But then the portrayal of mistress in residence back at the apartment had been spot on, too. They'd had a good three days to decide how to play this.

'How do I know you're telling the truth now? Did he put you up to this because he wants to keep me sweet? You did suggest it?' Zoe reminded tersely, not knowing what to think or believe any more. 'A way to keep my future wealth wedded to his.'

She felt Javier stiffen. She'd pricked that monumental pride of his. He'd hate to see his murky motives displayed. She should be experiencing triumph, vindication. So why did she want to cry?

'Tell her what you were doing in our apartment,' Javier demanded, contempt in his voice. Contempt for her or for Glenda, Zoe had no way of knowing.

Glenda shot him a look full of fury. 'That's between you and me. It's none of her business!'

'When you lied to my wife you made it her business.'

'You were going to give me money!' Glenda spat, hectic spots of colour high on her cheeks. 'I was broke and homeless, I had no one else to turn to. Then that overgrown schoolgirl who calls herself your wife walked in and threw a tantrum! I would make you a far better wife!'

'In your dreams,' Javier stated with contempt. 'So, broke and homeless, thrown out by your married French lover, you grabbed the opportunity to lie your head off, break up my marriage, then hang around long enough to console me for my wife's desertion,' Javier completed. 'I want to hear you admit it.'

Silence. Javier released Zoe's wrist and lifted his arm to lay it around her shoulders. Her legs felt hollow and she leant against him, grateful for the support. Had she misjudged him so badly?

'Well?' he pressed darkly, tacking on for good measure, 'Do I have to remind you of that cheque?'

Glenda gave him a look of sullen rage then spat out, 'OK, I admit it! Satisfied?' She stumped off towards his waiting car. 'Take me to that damned hotel—I've had enough of this!'

Five minutes later, Glenda and her suitcase deposited in the foyer of a country hotel, Javier turned a brief glance on Zoe as he returned to the driver's seat. 'Home now.'

The classic lines of his profile were grim. Her stomach flipped. She might have been naive in misjudging him, in accepting everything Glenda had said as the truth, but there were too many things left unspoken, so much she didn't know, the foremost amongst them being the way he saw their relation-ship.

And he was saying nothing, just firing the ignition. She felt light-headed with stress and said in a breathy little voice she barely recognised as her own, 'Take me back to Jenny's to pick up my car.'

Javier's hands tightened on the wheel as the Jaguar smoothly exited the hotel car park. 'We'll collect it in the morning. Until then I'm not letting you out of my sight. It's time the real truth came out,' he added grimly.

Having no idea what he meant by that, unless it had something to do with his relationship with the hateful Glenda, reminded her of something. 'Why did it take you from Monday to Thursday to decide to haul that woman here to make her confession?'

His long mouth tightened. They'd passed through the village and he was taking the lanes out to Wakeham at speed. 'It took me approximately three hours, not three days,' he gave back on an exasper-ated snap, slowing right down to take a particularly tight bend then powering on. 'Leave it for now.'

Good advice, Zoe had to admit, fiddling edgily with the strap of her seat belt. Clearly she was angering him, but never one to take orders easily she had to ask, 'Was Glenda with you in Cannes?'

'I met up with her there,' was the rawly given ad-mission as he turned into Wakeham's long driveway, shocking Zoe back into silent misery, struggling to discover where the truth lay in all this mess.

Keeping her silent, a hand pressed in the small of

her back, he urged her past Joe who was doing the evening rounds and checking the windows were closed, ignoring the older man's stunned expression, marching her to the master suite.

'Right,' he gritted as he closed the door behind them. 'I'm sick of playing games with our marriage.' Tension pulled his bronzed skin tight over his impressive features, his narrowed eyes almost black, glittering with what she had to translate as rage.

'Sick of pretending I had to work away from home just to move out of temptation's way. Sick of acting like a real nice considerate guy when all I wanted to do was rip your clothes off and make love to you. Sick of suffering agonies of guilt because I might have made you pregnant, beating myself up,' he emphasised with a savage bite. 'So I'm telling you here and now that I love you. I want to make this marriage work, I want to give you children. I want to tie you so closely to me you'll never escape!'

Zoe flopped down on the bed, her mouth dropping open. As a declaration of love it wouldn't win any awards in the sensitivity and hearts-and-flowers stakes but it was all she needed—everything she needed.

Tears of sheer happiness sprang to her eyes as he stalked to where she was sitting, thrusting his rigid face in front of hers, impatience with her poleaxed silence etched on every dominant feature. 'Well?'

She took his face between her hands and kissed him. At that precise moment it was the only answer she could give him. When his mouth returned the pressure of her lips with driven passion she knew her response to his question had been the right one. As he tumbled her back on the bed she felt the tremors that shook him as her arms closed around him, the heat of his virile body sending her flying on a giant wave of sensual excitement.

'I've always loved you,' Zoe managed at last to murmur against his erotically probing mouth. 'Since I was little,' she explained raggedly as he slowly lifted his head. 'Then the feeling changed,' she told his questing smoky eyes. 'I loved you as a woman. I fell fathoms-deep in love with you. I told you, remember, and embarrassed us both.'

Moving her hand from where it lay tucked against his thundering heartbeat, she lovingly traced the line of his hard, sensual mouth with the tips of her fingers. 'You probably thought it was a teenage infatuation. It wasn't,' she confirmed softly. 'It just grew and grew. Why else did you imagine I would ever agree to the sort of marriage you proposed? Kiss me again.'

With a low groan Javier obeyed the best order he'd ever been given, fingers tangling in her bright hair, disposing of the pins that held it in driven haste, one hand rucking up the skirt of her dress to press her hips against the hard evidence of his arousal, and it was a long time before either of them had the breath to spare for speech.

A long time before the break of the early summer dawn, long hours of mindblowing pleasure, of immeasurable ecstasy. And the words were drowsy when they came, Javier's hand lovingly stroking her tumbled hair from her damp forehead as he murmured, 'We need breakfast. Got to keep our strength up.' Smoky eyes glinted an explicit message that needed no verbal translation and Zoe ran her hands over the impressive breadth of his satin-skinned power-packed shoulders, dizzy with love for him, silently vowing to make him happy for the rest of his life.

'Patience,' he adjured softly, swinging his long legs off the bed, allowing her to just adore the smooth length of his bronzed back. 'I'll forage before Ethel surfaces.'

And then he was gone, leaving her to wonder how she could ever have doubted him, how she could ever have believed Glenda's vicious lies, knowing she was far too happy to eat anything, ever again!

But the combined aromas of fresh coffee and hot buttered toast swiftly changed her mind, and having him taste her warm buttery lips with his own was something out of this world and definitely to be repeated every time they breakfasted together.

Which reminded her. 'May I take it that you won't be dashing away all over the world on business without me in future?'

'You may.' His charismatic grin flooded her with warmth. 'I admit to poking my unnecessary nose into far-flung projects because every time I looked at you I wanted to make wild love to you, and our stupid marriage wasn't about that. I thought I was doing the honourable thing. And while we're on the subject of mixed-up wiring—where did you get the crazy idea that I'd proposed to you to—what did you call it? Get wedded to your future fortune?'

Finishing the last of her coffee, Zoe dismissed her

folly as lightly as possible. 'Something Glenda said.' She wasn't about to drag his mother into this; she would hate to cause any ill feeling.

Javier took the empty cup from her hand and leaned over to put it on the tray at the bedside, his voice gruff as he eased himself closer to the sinful temptation of her beautiful body. 'Didn't you stop to think? If I'd wanted to marry your money, scatter-brain, I would never have proposed a two-year paper marriage in the first place. And as for the other charge you threw at me, Glenda and I didn't sit around for half a week deciding whether or not she should face you with what she'd done.'

He hoisted himself up on one elbow, the better to devour her lovely face with his greedy eyes. 'Though, thinking about it, I can't blame you. Something that did require the presence of my poking nose did crop up the day after I got back to the apartment after leaving you with your grandmother. A suspension-bridge project on the outskirts of Milan.

'I phoned through to warn you I'd be out of the country until Thursday—yesterday. You were with Alice and her GP. I asked Miss Pilkington to pass on the message. She forgot to, as I discovered when I phoned to let you know I was back yesterday mid-morning. When she told me you'd left for the London apartment on the previous Monday I went cold all over and guessed you'd walked in and found Glenda. It only needed the threat to stop the cheque I'd given her to get her to confess to what had happened.'

He moved closer, stroking a hand over her swollen, sensitised breasts, a hard thigh insinuating itself between the limpid length of hers. 'I think I have my strength back, my darling.'

Stifling a moan of need, Zoe wriggled away. 'There are a couple of things I need to know,' she stated emphatically, then gasped with helpless excitement as he hauled her back again. 'What was that woman doing in our apartment and why did you give her money?' she got out in breathy stabs as his roving hands found the hot, melting core of her.

'Oh, that.' He, too, was having difficulty in the breathing department. She was so sweet, so soft, so ready, so adored—

'Yes. That.' Her futile attempt to push him away turned into an eager exploration of her own.

Calling on his last remnants of self-control, Javier got out, 'Just after I called you from the hotel reception area in Cannes—I was waiting for the site manager—a working dinner—who should swan up but that wretched woman on the arm of her French lover. Then, when we were in Spain, Mama told me she'd been trying to get in touch with me. I thought nothing more of it until that first day back at the apartment I found a message from her on the phone. She sounded pretty desperate so I returned the call. She was almost incoherent. She'd been dumped, ejected from the flat the French guy had installed her in. Was homeless, fast running out of money, would I advance her a loan until she got back on her feet.'

His mouth hardened. With hindsight he should have told her to get lost. But he'd been sympathetic.

'I felt sorry for her. We'd had a brief fling, way in the past, no strings, no come-backs. But after it was over she had done me favours in return for payment—accompanying you on those trips abroad when I'd been too busy pitching for new projects to spare the time. By then I knew I'd be flying out to Milan on the following morning so I told her to go to the apartment, and to ask the janitor, on the instruction I gave him, to let her in if for some reason you and I weren't there. Wanting somewhere to lay her lying head, she obviously moved in. The rest you know. Or is there anything else before I explode with frustration?'

He smiled but it was the smile of a jungle cat just about to pounce on its prey. Zoe loved it. Loved him and everything about him to pieces.

Tilting her head on one side, she squirmed against him. 'Just one more question. Have you really got your strength back?'

His ragged groan, the expertise with which he lowered his mouth to kiss her senseless, were the perfect answer to her question.

The world's bestselling romance series.

HARLEQUIN®
Presents

Seduction and Passion Guaranteed!

OUTBACK KNIGHTS
Marriage is their mission!

From bad boys—to powerful,
passionate protectors!

Three tycoons from the Outback
rescue their brides-to-be....

**Coming soon in Harlequin Presents:
Emma Darcy's exciting new trilogy**

Meet Ric, Mitch and Johnny—once three Outback bad
boys, now rich and powerful men. But these sexy city
tycoons must return to the Outback to face a new
challenge: claiming their women as their brides!

**MAY 2004: THE OUTBACK MARRIAGE RANSOM #2391
JULY 2004: THE OUTBACK WEDDING TAKEOVER #2403
NOVEMBER 2004: THE OUTBACK BRIDAL RESCUE #2427**

*"Emma Darcy delivers a spicy love story...
a fiery conflict and a hot sensuality."*
—Romantic Times

Available wherever Harlequin books are sold.

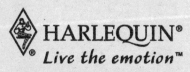

HARLEQUIN®
Live the emotion™

Visit us at www.eHarlequin.com

HPEDARCY

Harlequin Romance®

THE WEDDING PLANNERS

Where weddings are all in a day's work!

Have you ever wondered about the women behind the scenes, the ones who make those special days happen, the ones who help to create a memory built on love that lasts forever—who, no matter how expert they are at helping others, can't quite sort out their love lives for themselves?

Meet Tara, Skye and Riana—three sisters whose jobs consist of arranging the most perfect and romantic weddings imaginable—and read how they find themselves walking down the aisle with their very own Mr. Right...!

Don't miss the THE WEDDING PLANNERS trilogy by Australian author Darcy Maguire:

A Professional Engagement HR#3801

On sale June 2004 in Harlequin Romance®!

Plus:

The Best Man's Baby, HR#3805, on sale July 2004
A Convenient Groom, HR#3809, on sale August 2004

Available at your favorite retail outlet.

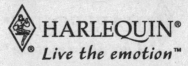

HARLEQUIN®
Live the emotion™

Visit us at www.eHarlequin.com

HRTWP

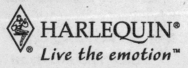

"Joanna Wayne weaves together a romance and suspense with pulse-pounding results!"
—*New York Times* bestselling author Tess Gerritsen

National bestselling author

JOANNA WAYNE

Alligator Moon

Determined to find his brother's killer, John Robicheaux finds himself entangled with investigative reporter Callie Havelin. Together they must shadow the sinister killer slithering in the murky waters—before they are consumed by the darkness....

A riveting tale that shouldn't be missed!

Coming in June 2004.

HARLEQUIN®

Live the emotion™

Visit us at www.eHarlequin.com

PHAM

If you enjoyed what you just read,
then we've got an offer you can't resist!

Take 2 bestselling
love stories FREE!
Plus get a FREE surprise gift!

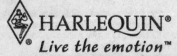